MIND BLOWER

I WAS LED into one of the rooms at the back of the house. It had nothing in it but a bed, and seemed to be little used. I was made to undress, and was then tied to the bed with silk cords. I tried to fight back, but was quickly discouraged by the bulk and efficiency of my captors. I wondered just what was in store, when a door opened, and Tocco entered, leading the seven young people I had just seen down at the stream.

MIND BLOWER

Marco Vassi

NEXUS
A NEXUS BOOK
published by
the Paperback Division of
W H Allen & Co plc

A Nexus Book
Published in 1990
by the Paperback Division of
W H Allen & Co. plc
Sekforde House, 175/9 St John Street
London EC1V 4LL

Printed and bound in Great Britain by
Cox & Wyman Ltd, Reading

ISBN 0 352 32692 1

For Ellen

with acknowledgements to
J. Krishnamurti
John Fowles

CHAPTER ONE

The fact that the ad was in the *Times* and not one of the sex journals made its wording all the more seductive: 'Wanted. Sensitive male to serve as personal valet and assistant to master in arcane studies.' A shiver of anticipation went through me as I dialled the number listed, and when a deeply female voice answered at the other end, all my senses were alert. I have overcome the prejudice against answering such requests when I realised that in a technological society the mass media served the equivalent purposes of court gossip in earlier times. She gave almost no information on the phone, and her questions seemed aimed to elicit responses that had more to do with what kind of person I was than what references I had. Of course, I wasn't really looking for a valet's job. I had wanted to get in touch with people who were playing serious sexual games, as I was tired of the hit-and-miss sort of thing that happens through cruising. I played a hunch.

'I feel like my character's being read,' I said.

There was a pause. 'One of the things Doctor Tocco studies is the language of human sounds. Sometimes it is much more rewarding to hear how a person moans than to listen to their theories of life. Don't you find?'

Either I was projecting my hope or she was laying out heavier cues than I had expected. A certain wet tension

,yed back and forth through the wires that had little to co with standard electricity. There was a silence, during which a good portion of my past sped at lightning speed through my mind.

I am not handsome in any conventional sense. Too short for movie-screen masculine appeal, nonetheless I am blessed with rich, curly black hair, a subtle olive complexion, and the Scorpio nature. Through an interesting genetic quirk, I have an embryonic third nipple on the right side of my chest, a sign of passion among Mediterranean people. In all, my dominant vibration is sex.

I had long ago stopped counting how many men and women I'd been to bed with, and in how many combinations. Physical conquest was easy enough, and after a while I learned to shelve any emotional complications so that I always entered and exited clean. But except for very rare cases, there had always been a quality of intellect missing, an ability to join my partner or partners in fucking the same fantasy. No matter how often we came together with our bodies, I had never shared an image orgasm with anyone. And countless times, while sinking into comfortable semi-slumber with a satisfied fellow human animal, discontent still whipped through my mind like a winter wind, until I came to despair of ever knowing total union with anyone. Occasionally I would attempt some quasi-therapeutic approach, where both of us free-associated how we balled, but these efforts became so solemn that they ended in giggles. Yet somewhere inside me I knew that others must be wrestling with the same problem, and I resolved to find them. It became a quest on the level of an apprentice seeking a master alchemist, only the crucibles I wanted to use were human beings.

A long series of efforts led me to New York City where I began the game that had been recommended to me by a vental Theosophist: waiting, with utmost, unrelenting awareness. 'Just stay tuned in to who you are and what you desire, and when you are ready, your teacher will appear,' he had said in the proper cryptic manner.

Already a number of avenues had opened, but they all turned out to be false starts, so I was trying not to be too excited about this one.

I snapped out of my reveries and answered her. 'A moan is usually solicited . . . under pressure,' I said, trying to conjure up images of leather thongs with the sound of my voice.

'If you understand that the only meaningful bondage is that which is entered into freely, you may want to meet Doctor Tocco,' she countered.

I successfully kept the tremor out of my voice as we set up the appointment.

From the outside the building was a solid, respectable, 19th-century reconstructed brownstone. As soon as I went in, however, I met with that rarest of experiences in the city – total silence. A plaque on the door read simply: ISM. When I closed it behind me I realised that the place was completely soundproofed. I was led in by a secretary who was pretty in that glossy kind of way girls who work in offices affect. But she was barefoot and wore a great mu-mu that covered everything but her hands and head. It was made of a clinging material that stuck like plastic wrap to various parts of her body as she moved. It was clear that she had nothing on underneath, and by the time we reached the end of the hall I knew the size and shape of her nipples, her buttocks, her bellybutton. I got only a fuzzy flash of her face, fascinated as I was by the continual shifting array of body parts singled out for attention by the movement of the dress. As we got to the door to which I was being led, my mouth was dry, and when she turned to open the door I inclined my head a few inches to see if the cloth had caught between her legs. But just then a booming male voice called out, 'Our young visitor wishes to see your cunt, Susan. Lift your skirt, please.'

I was stunned by the double shock, first of having my barely perceptible gesture not only seen but announced out loud, and then of watching the girl at my side pull her dress up over her waist. I wanted to see who the man in

11

office was, but I was mesmerised by the sight of a totally hairless cunt pouting between two very full thighs. I looked up at her face and was astonished to see she was blushing. Everything had proceeded with such rapidity that I didn't, until that moment, realise what an odd situation this was! It was all I could do to keep from reaching over and putting my hand on that soft totally naked pussy.

I heard a large scraping sound and turned just in time to see what looked like a modern Sidney Greenstreet hoisting himself out of his chair. He was a huge man, almost six feet tall and perhaps weighing three hundred pounds, sporting a walrus moustache and bushy side-burns, wearing a tailored satin jumpsuit in glowing psychadelic colours. He held out one hand, and as I shook it he said, 'My name is Tocco. I have been looking forward to meeting you.'

He led me towards his desk and I glanced back at Susan, who still stood there with her dress up. 'Come along, Susan,' he said. 'Stand where our friend can see you.' He sat me down in a chair facing his desk and Susan came to stand in front of it; now she pulled the skirt up so that her face was covered and I was presented with the sight of her breasts as well, placed high on her chest and hanging so that the upper surface was as delicately curved as a ski slope, and the underpart dropped like a ripe pear. Her nipples pointed up and were slightly wrinkled.

Tocco sat down. 'I have dispensed with the formalities because I am certain you are the man I want. I have been informed by a number of my people that you have been seriously *searching* for some time now.' And he put an odd, Ouspenskyesque intonation on the word that set my head spinning. 'Our centre is composed of people who have already passed through most of the preliminary states of sexual exploration and are ready for life.'

The conversation was already going a bit too fast, and I interjected, 'What does ISM stand for?'

He smiled. 'Ah. That is the Institute for Sexual Meth-atheatre. We shall discuss the meaning of that title later.

12

But for now, let us examine a specific example.' He stood up and in brisk professional tones continued. 'The problem is, of course, that one tires very quickly of the variations on the physical. It is necessary to be free of the tyranny of form before form can be freely appreciated. Here at ISM we get very quickly to the point where no physical activity is considered peculiar or special in any way. And then we examine the psychological underpinnings. Take Susan for example.' He turned to her. 'Kneel!' He said. She knelt down. 'Now, let us have your mouth.'

With that she dropped the dress from her face; she opened her mouth and began running her tongue over her lips, then sticking her tongue out as far as it would go, and then letting her lips quiver as though she were imploring. 'Sound!' said Tocco. She began moaning and begging. 'Give it to me, please give it to me! I want it in the mouth!'

My first reaction was an erection, which Doctor Tocco leaned over the desk to look at as it bulged through my pants. 'Well, take it out,' he said. 'Come on.'

I hesitated.

'See here. We have no time for foolishness. If you are going to waste time with social amenities, we'll never get down to the real work. If you want to assist me, you must immediately drop all conditioning and understand that sex is a tool, a function of your consciousness. If you confuse it with personality and social roles, we'll just be playing silly games.'

It was the first time I had been given a lecture while sitting with an erection in front of a moaning girl who was imploring me to give it to her in the mouth. But, of course, he was right. And upon realising that, I felt a sudden lightheartedness. I was in the presence of peers, people such as I had been looking for a long time. At last there was someone who could help me with the problem of fantasy fucking. I stood up, unzipped my fly, and let a seven-inch, gnarled, competent, wise, gentle, ruthless, purple-crowned cock flip out.

13

...cco looked at it for a few seconds with professional ...iration. 'Excellent,' he said. 'Now to the girl.'

He walked behind Susan and pulled the dress up completely over her head so that she was totally naked. 'She has achieved only a middle-level mindlessness, but is progressing well. From her accounts she has attained four actual instances of sexual satori, but as well we know, enlightenment is only a signpost to let us know how much harder we have to work.' He bent over her and whispered, 'Lie down, Susan, take it on your back.' She keeled over with a sob, and lay writhing on the floor. Her mouth was working more convulsively than ever. She began licking the air with her tongue.

'Much of this is role actualisation,' he said, 'and it's interesting that . . .' But I was transfixed, watching her. 'Oh,' he said, 'excuse me. By all means, help yourself.'

I was past all attempts to figure it out. My only focus was to get my cock into her mouth. I kneeled down with my knees on either side of her head, and leaned forward. Immediately she reached up and took it as far as it would go into her mouth, and then made a gulping movement which drove it down into her throat. At that her legs kicked up and a look of unbearable pain and ecstasy came over her face. She pulled back just as quickly and lay there gasping. She seemed helpless, and that very help-lessness made me want to violate her further. This time I drove into her throat until I could feel her gulping on the head of my cock. She fought free and turned her head aside. I wondered whether I had hurt her, but she turned back and pushed herself lower, until she had taken my balls in her mouth. She began a frantic licking deep between my thighs until, with a deep cry, she took my arsehole full onto her mouth, and then started working her tongue into it.

I looked up. The doctor was smiling. 'It's quite aston-ishing. She will lick, suck, swallow, kiss, or nibble on anything you put into her mouth. Toes, urine, faeces. Would you like to pee in her mouth, my young friend?'

Simultaneously, Susan moved forward and was taking

the head of my cock on to her tongue as waves of paranoia were emanating from Doctor Tocco. I was torn between a sense of infinitely sickening ugliness and profound release. The thin line between insanity and holiness was stretched to the breaking point, and I had either to drop all the labels and all preconceptions and dive into the mix, or else deal with the frightening judgements which were beginning to swim up from my social conscience.

'You see,' Tocco went on relentlessly. 'It is a very complex affair. And we have just begun. Are you sure you want to go on, to pursue this knowledge, into the mysteries of sex and its partner, death, to follow the terrifying paths of beauty and terror to their final end?'

And as all the shades of ambivalence raced through my mind like great spectral horses, Susan began panting and slobbering and crying greedily, 'Fuck me, fuck me in the mouth, give it to me, anything, feed me, anything, in my mouth, open, shoot it, suck it, me, oh, oohhh-ohhh!' Her breasts were crushed between my thighs, her body writhing beneath me. Her open wet red mouth crying to be filled grabbed me from the horns of my metaphysical dilemma, and I sank, halfway between longing and disgust, into her throat. She sucked at my cock like a whirlpool, and I could feel myself being drawn out from my arsehole and the pit of my stomach and my chest. I looked down and saw her now wild face pressed full against the black pubic hair and every last inch of cock was totally imbedded deep in the recesses of her mouth. Everything cut loose inside me, and my orgasm boiled over; I shot spasm after spasm of hot sperm into her, crying: 'Yes, yes, yes!'

I rode it for many long seconds and then fell forward on my elbows. She lay quiet, and as my cock grew smaller she lapped it gently with her tongue, licking off the last drops of sperm which dribbled out and then sucking it clean.

The room resounded with a great silence, and Tocco cleared his throat to speak.

'Good. I like to see the young people enjoy themselves.' And he laughed in a deep baritone which couldn't help but make one feel that all had to be right with the world.

I stood up, and for a moment felt awkward. Tocco had already gone back to some paperwork at his desk, and it was as though I had been dismissed. There was a stirring under me and Susan got to her feet. I was almost afraid to look at her, but when I did I was greeted by a warm, appreciative smile, and a pair of intelligent and lively grey eyes.

'Hello,' she said. 'I'm glad you'll be working with us. I think we'll get along very well.' She reached down and threw her dress over herself once more. 'Come on,' she said, walking out. 'I'll show you to your room.'

CHAPTER TWO

The room was indistinguishable from any you might find in a modern motel. I was somewhat worried about clothing, but the closet held a number of shirts and trousers and jackets of various sizes. I felt as though I was entering a monastery, ready to throw off all vestiges of my old life, and I decided on the spot not even to go back to tie up loose ends on the 'outside'.

Susan showed me around and then left. I undressed, showered, and settled down for a good night's sleep. On the table next to the bed was a small pamphlet which seemed be privately published. The cover bore the simple inscription: ISM. I flipped it open at random, and found it to be a dense philosophical polemic on the nature of reality and illusion, and the role of sex in man's attainment of cosmic consciousness. It had illustrations from some ancient Tibetan tracts on Tantric Yoga. I was in the middle of deciding whether I should look for some other reading material, when I heard a light knock at the door.

'Come in,' I yelled, expecting Tocco or Susan. The door swung open and there stood a perfectly beautiful young girl of about nineteen. She was quite thin, with almost nonexistent breasts, narrow hips, and a boyish cast to her posture. Her hair was long to her waist and a shimmering golden brown. She had eyes like almonds, and a wide, full mouth. She wore a totally transparent negligee, and the dark of her nipples and pubic hair were like shadows at the bottom of a fish pond. She lifted one leg, and I saw she had that rare quality in a woman's body where the thighs do not join snugly at the crotch, but rise like pillars into the torso and leave a space between them of several inches. That yawning gap, hanging like a stone bridge across a chasm, was her cunt, made by nature to be wide and open and accessible.

'Come in,' I said again, more quietly this time. She smiled and her face was total mockery. 'You would like that, wouldn't you?' she taunted. I looked again and ran my tongue over my lips. 'More than you can imagine,' I said.

'Well, let's leave imagination out of it. What are you willing to do?'

For a moment I missed the intent of her words, and then I remembered what the scene was in the building. This must be some sort of test, I thought. Deliberately, and without removing my eyes from hers, I threw back the covers on the bed and exposed my body. I reached down with my right hand and grabbed my cock. Slowly, languorously. I began stroking it. It stirred gently, and then began to get hard. I pulled on it more purposefully, and it came to its full length and width. I looked down at the hard tool, and then back at her. 'It's not what I am willing to do to let you in, but what are you willing to do for me to allow you in.' She turned sideways and made as if to go, but stopped and looked down and back over her shoulder. I followed the line of sight and beheld perhaps the most perfectly-formed arse I had ever seen in my life. It lay in perfect proportion to the rest of her body, and then was just a little larger than scale. The buttocks broke right at the tops of her thighs, and rounded out in full globes. A deep, rich cleft offered an enternity of explora-tion. She arched her back, and her arse rose high and away, inviting, opening. Simultaneously she ran her tongue over her lips and brought one hand down between her legs. With great delicacy she put one finger into her cunt, bringing the material of her gown with it.

Clearly she had more ammunition than I did for this war of nerves, but I had more muscle. I got out of bed, walked slowly over to her, and before she could react, grabbed her and swung her up over my shoulders. She started to kick and protest, but I threw her ungracefully down on the bed and landed on top of her. We wrestled furiously. Her anger was genuine, and matched my lust.

Gradually my weight began to wear her down, and in a few moments she lay exhausted and panting under me. Holding her her wrists together with one hand, I reached down and ripped the negligee off. She was even more breathtaking up close. Her skin was dimensional; to touch her lightly was to sink into a pool of sensations. I relaxed and just drank it all in. The breasts lay flattened against her rib cage, and from the waist up she might have been a boy. The thought inflamed me and for a moment I felt a spark fly from her mind to mine. Without thinking I reached forward and took one nipple in my mouth. The effect was electrifying. All her bravado melted away instantaneously and she twisted her torso up to force the nipple deeper into my mouth. I cupped her breast and bunched it together, making it seem larger than it was, and then took the entire thing in my mouth as though it were a small peach. Gently I dug my teeth into her and lapped with my tongue at the warm flesh which filled my mouth. She grabbed my hair and pulled my head down, forcing me to go even more deeply into her.

We stayed locked like that for a long moment, and then I pulled back. At the same time she let go, and we lay for a while unmoving, my head on her chest, listening to the pounding of her heart. In a while there was within us both some kind of stirring. And once again I began to move, but now I went towards her mouth. She reached for me greedily, and before my lips reached hers she began licking my mouth and face. Her tongue was sensitive and quick, and I closed my eyes and let it roam over my eyes and forehead and cheeks. Finally she reached around and inserted the tip of her tongue into my ear, something which is like pushing the red alert inside me. I moved on

21

reflex and reached down to plant my hand square between her thighs in the space between cunt and arsehole. I grabbed her hard and perhaps hurt her a little bit, but she moaned and fell back writhing. I moved down and sat directly between her legs. I pushed her thighs apart and looked long and lovingly at the already wet cunt before me.

It was a heartbreakingly beautiful picture. Dark matted hair, red-violet lips, white flesh, and dark folds underneath where the buttocks met. And the entire thing resting on a firm globular arse, the curves of which peeked out from under as she lay there. To make it even more heady, the pungent aroma of cunt was already beginning to fill the air.

I reached forward with both hands and parted the outer lips. The inner lips were still stuck together, pink and closed, and gently I ran my finger down between them until they too fell open. She responded with a deep, ecstatic sigh and I saw a shudder of acceptance go through her entire body. I leaned forward and peered at the very heart of her cunt, and the rose-bud opening which lay buried under all the protective layers. I inserted my middle finger and was immediately plunged into a different world, a world where variations in heat and texture were the only language. My feelings varied between the clinical and the poetic. At one point I was touching and identifying all the anatomical parts, and suddenly I was only deep in wet, pulsating cunt, with an exquisite young woman reacting to my every touch with silent implorings to have me do more.

I reached the cervix and touched the very entrance to the womb. She gasped and I pulled out my finger, only to insert my hand. I put all four fingers from thumb to ring finger into the cunt opening. At first she resisted, but I moved in without hurting her, and soon I was in her as far as anatomy would allow. I let my hand loose and just walked and stroked and pinched every inch of her now-stretched cunt. She reached down and, kicking up her legs, grabbed her ankles so that she was completely split

22

apart, totally exposed. The juices were running very freely and dribbling down between her buttocks. I twisted my hand enough to allow me to put my pinky into her arsehole, now lubricated by her own secretions. All the barriers broke at once, and I found myself in a frenzy of movement, pushing and pulling and twisting and pummelling her cunt and arse, not knowing whether I was hurting her or giving her pleasure, and hearing from a distance her cries of desire, screaming for more and more, until the spasms began deep in her cunt and moved down into her belly, and she rocked and came and came.

She fell back, eyes closed, and didn't move. I slowly pulled my hand out of her, and looked at the thin wild body now lying so still. For an instant she seemed dead, and the thought excited me beyond my expectations. That was one trip it seemed I would never enjoy. But she was alive, and I could pretend she was dead. Thus having my cake and talk to it too. I moved up and stretched myself out over her. 'Don't move,' I said. 'I want you to lie perfectly still. Don't make a sound. I'm going to shove my cock into you, and fuck you until I come. And you're going to lie there and take it. I don't care whether you like it or not. I'm not interested in anything except your cunt right now.'

I lowered myself on to her and felt my cock immediately sink into the sticky hot pussy. It was a paradisal as I expected. The natural space between her thighs made her cunt like a snug harbour. There was nothing between me and total penetration. I pushed all the way in, and then out. I moved the tip of my cock around the fringes of the outer lips. I teased at the cunt hole, and then rammed violently in. I moved from side to side, came in at a dozen different angles. And only when I got in from above, rubbing her clitoris with the shaft of my cock as the head penetrated her, did she move. It was an involuntary spasm, but that tiny response was more exciting than most of the thrashing around that is usually done. I kept riding her high until the tension mounted past her ability to control, and she opened her legs wider, pulled her knees

23

up to her chest, and exposed the deepest part of her box. I drove all the way in, to that spot where the symbolic virginity perpetually lies, and rode home until the hot sperm spilled out of me and splashed against the walls of the inside of her body.

Unexpectedly, as I lay in her arms, I fell into a peaceful sleep, and when I woke up a half hour later, we were in exactly the same position. My cock was still inside her. I roused myself and stretched my cramped limbs a bit, and she stirred too. We gingerly disengaged our bodies and sat up.

I looked at her for a long time. She seemed even younger now. 'What's your name?' I asked. 'Anita,' she said. There didn't seem to be too much else to say.

'You're new here, aren't you?' she asked. I lit a cigarette. 'Yes, and you?'

'I've been here . . . quite a while.'

There was something very odd about the way she spoke, as though she weren't really interested in herself or in me or anything. 'When did you come here?' I asked. 'What brought you?'

She laughed, nervously. 'The stork brought me.'

'No, really,' I implored.

'It's true,' she said. 'I was born here. Doctor Tocco is my father.'

My eyes bugged out. 'Your father! And you mean he lets you . . . I mean . . . do you . . . I . . .' I trailed off.

'It's all right,' she said, 'sex isn't a bad thing. And I like it. But . . .'

'But what?'

She drew a long soulful breath. 'It gets kind of boring after a while, doesn't it?'

'Well,' I said, getting polemical, 'that's the purpose of the research here, isn't it? To solve the problems of boredom? Besides, you didn't seem bored a half hour ago.'

She grew very sad. 'No, it's always exciting the first time with someone. But I want to be able to stay with somebody. I want to get married and have children. want a man that I can love all the time.'

Poor Tocco, I thought. Here he is with the world's most far-out sexual scene going, and his daughter wants to live in a house with a white picket fence, cooking and fucking for a nine-to-fiver, when she chould have the pick of any kind of relationship she wanted.

I felt kind of sorry for her, even though I didn't begin to understand the complexities of the situation, and had no desire to go into them. It all seemed too much like a Gothic soap-opera. To be polite I asked, 'Well, why don't you leave?'

She looked at me and my scalp tingled as I got a precognition flash on what she was going to say before the words were out of her mouth. 'I can't,' she answered. 'He won't let me out.'

'You must be joking,' I said.

'You too,' she responded. 'You can't get out either.'

I looked wildly around the room. Of course, that was the odd thing that had bothered me without my being able to put a finger on it. There was no window. And the building was soundproofed. I started to get up but she put an arm on my shoulder. 'Believe me,' she said flatly, 'you can't.' And I believed her, for her tone was that of someone who is telling an unpleasant but necessary truth.

What kind of man is Tocco? I wondered. But my thought was distracted by a sensation, and I focused in to see Anita leaning over and swishing her long silken hair over my thighs. Slowly she lowered her head further and further until her hair lay like a sandpile on my legs, and then I felt her warm, lush mouth cover my genitals entirely. And as her tongue began lapping at the base of my cock, the erection began to grow and throb with anticipation.

I lay back and let her suck me off while I pondered my strange situation. Perhaps Tocco was a madman, but there was nothing to do about it now. If I were to be shot in the morning, I might as well enjoy the night. And I

25

turned all my attention to the beautiful face which seemed to be staring with such intensity at my pubic hair as the mouth moved in easy glides up and down the shaft of my prick.

CHAPTER THREE

The following morning brought anxiety. After Anita left I lay in bed for a while, and then prowled the corridor. The door to the downstairs was solid oak and bolted shut. The other rooms on the floor were similar to mine, but I only got a dim impression of their contents, since the light switches weren't functional. Some seemed to be outfitted with leather couches, mirrors and videotape equipment; others were either totally bare or covered from wall to wall with mattresses; one looked like a miniaturised laboratory. At one point a door opened and Susan came out into the hall. Her hair was dishevelled and her nightgown was obviously just thrown on in haste. I sensed that there was someone in her room, and for an instant, I felt a totally irrational pang of jealousy and possessiveness. She looked at me oddly, then said, 'I heard doors opening and closing.'

I tried my best cheerful manner. 'Just looking around,' I said. I edged towards her door, feeling slightly malicious. 'Uh, is it too late for us to have a drink and talk?'

She fixed me with a long hard stare. 'Don't play games, Michael. I am in the first stages of fucking someone, and your knocking around out here has interrupted it, and I don't feel like a threesome tonight.' I smiled, and it felt like a mule shitting thistles. 'No need to get touchy, Susan.' She shook her hair out. 'I'm always annoyed when men are coy.' And with that she went back inside and slammed the door shut.

I stood around foolishly for a while, and then decided that there was nothing I could do about anything, and went to bed where I began counting backwards from a million until I fell asleep. When I woke up there was not the slightest indication of what time it was, but my internal clock told me it must be around ten. I began going through my catatonic dialogue, in which the intellect attempts to convince the body that there is a valid reason for getting up, and the body lies there knowing full well that the notion of activity is a prejudice best done away with. This morning the conversation became unusually dull, the body was about to win by filibuster, and I began dozing back off to sleep.

Suddenly the door burst open. I sat up and saw an eerie sight. It was Tocco, dressed in spangled Bermuda shorts, flanked by two absolutely beautiful men. One was tall, black, and deeply-muscled, while the other was pale white, thin, and soft as a deer. Behind them came Susan, dressed as a nurse, carrying a tray of vials, syringes, vapourisers and small bottles. They sailed in majestically.

Tocco was his usual exuberant self. 'If you are at all normal, Michael,' he began, 'you are now in a state of anxiety and suspicion. You are convinced that I am a madman who has locked you in to wreak strange tortures upon you. And in one sense, that interpretation is entirely correct. You may feel your mind slipping. And that is just as it should be. Our intention this morning is, in fact, to give it a little push. Your worst habit is this constant effort to rationalise things, to figure them out. As though the universe made sense! A preposterous preoccupation.'

I started to protest that I hadn't even told him why I had come to ISM, but my efforts were brushed aside. The four of them surrounded the bed, and I twisted my head frantically, trying to read some kind of intent in their eyes. The two strange men, at a signal from Tocco, took off their clothes and came to sit on either side of me on the bed. I realised that I could, at any moment, jump up and be free, but morbid curiosity riveted me to the spot. A kind of powerlessness overcame me, and although I knew that I had control, pretending to lose that control sent a thrill of sexual undercurrent through my body.

'Lie back, Michael,' Tocco said. 'You are still half asleep, still in dreams. Not only this morning, but through your entire life. You get through your days and you have flashes of insight, but you are not yet able to perceive things as they are. Now, outside this building, the sun is shining, and civilisation is making its rounds, but here we have cancelled time; the only time which exists is the rise and fall of desire.' I closed my eyes and the words washed over me like waves. 'Here, there is only desire . . . overwhelming, blind, endless, insatiable desire. And you are its manifestation, its slave.'

As he spoke, Susan slipped a hypodermic needle into my arm, and I felt the first speed flash almost before I could flinch. The great rush of indescribable bliss poured through me. I was flushed with longing, with an immense love which expanded through all space and embraced everything that existed in the entire universe. My arms and legs became heavy and my skin grew sensitive to the air; I lay back open, uncaring, ready to accept whatever the universe wanted to give.

I felt hands, many hands, begin to caress my body. I didn't know whose they were and it didn't matter. It was flesh, it was alive, it was wanting. Lips came down and covered my mouth, and a large, rough tongue worked its way under my lips, around my teeth, into my cheeks, on my own tongue. The mouth was insistent, hungry, and I was ready to give it everything.

Simultaneously, hands parted my legs, and fingers groped between the cheeks of my arse. I couldn't restrain myself, writhing, yearning, moving. Teeth bit at my nipples with little tearing bites, hurting but not damaging, almost damaging, sending waves of sensitive resistance through me. Then they moved down, gnawing at my ribs.

Another mouth covered my cock and began sucking, pulling, lapping. I was spent with spasms of ecstasy. All

31

the sensations merged, and suddenly I flashed a high stone altar at noon under a scorching sun. Aztec priests chanted over the sacrifice; their great gold mantles shone like fire. Below, ten thousand people roared, and that roar blended with the pounding in my ears. I was the sacrifice; I was the body being offered, the flesh which was being torn and eaten. I was smothered with bodies and breath and movement. I laughed in triumph. Willingly I gave myself. Let the stone knife penetrate my bowels. I heard myself moaning, 'Give it to me, do it, do it, fuck me, kill me, eat me, give it to me, yes, yes . . .'

Then everyone suddenly pulled back and stood again by the side of the bed, coldly, quietly. It was as though they had thrown cold water on me. I opened my eyes, unbelieving. I felt like a lunatic being objectively observed by psychiatrists. Immediately, I felt my nakedness, my physical nakedness, my psychological exposure. I was ashamed, and from the shame grew anger. And then I felt sick to my stomach. I began to get off the bed when Tocco put a restraining hand on my shoulder.

'Now, remember what you are here for.'

'I don't know what I'm here for!' I screamed. 'I wanted to find out more about sex, and I heard about this underground society. But now I'm locked in with a bunch of sadists, and being humiliated, and . . .' But I heard the sound of my voice, and I admitted to myself, much to my chagrin, that it was no different from that of a whining child. I subsided, and the feelings must have shown on my face, for Tocco said, 'Yes, I'm glad you saw it yourself. Of course you are to be humiliated. That is not the least of what will happen to you here. Do you think we have time to waste in simple orgies? *It is the shock which teaches*. And the shock does no good if you are expecting it, or are able to take it in stride. But we will save the theoretical discussion for later. For now, I want you to observe what a will-less puppet you are.'

With that the black man came up on to the bed and pushed me back down. He knelt with his knees at my ears. He had an enormous cock, even limp, and it hung over my face like a curved banana. The others watched. Inside me my emotions and the speed churned, and I was in no mood for sex. But he leaned forward and just barely touched the edges of my lips with the head of his cock. Immediately upon contact I succumbed. Desire grabbed me like a balled fist. I felt myself go soft, and then moved my head from side to side so my mouth would just touch the very sensitive opening in the tip of the prick, giving him the most exquisite of light sensations. The pressure in my chest increased.

I felt my face changed. I attempted to contact the inner feelings, and realised that I was suddenly sixteen, and a girl. I had become a skittish young virgin, much like the kind that I used to date, the kind whose defences provided their greatest source of eroticism. I realised that I was reliving a projection, and now I was to learn first-hand about those defences. But I would also have control. I was the dispenser of pleasure, and I could play with him as delicately as I wanted. Revelations surged through me as I put my tongue out ever so slightly and inserted it into the opening of his cock. I could hear him pull in his breath quickly. I moved down and put my tongue at the crack where thighs and balls meet, the most sensitive part.

Then I heard a snap, and the sweet smell of amyl nitrate filled the room. An inhalator was put into my nose, and as I breathed deeply, a voice said, 'Go down on him, baby, go all the way down. Lick him good.'

The drug unstrung me. Rush after rush of longing left me totally open. I clamped my mouth around his arsehole and sucked for all I was worth. Every fold of skin, every hair bristle, was a sharp sensation. Part of me saw the picture of myself lying with a man grinding his arse into my face, and myself loving it, wanting more, probing deeper. Decadence and liberty raced neck and neck. He reached back and spread his cheeks, and the hole pushed forward, as though he were going to shit in my mouth. But I was beyond caring. I was where it felt right doing what felt good. What did it matter what the forms were? I dug deep into his arsehole with my tongue and then licked him all over, up and down the crack and over every inch of the glistening cheeks. The deep musky smell made me drunk. I gasped and sucked pleasure from the opening.

Another realisation struck. I was sucking pleasure! Yet just a moment ago it was to have been I who gave pleasure. The image of a wizened succubus went through my mind. Whose pleasure was this? Was I the timid teenage girl allowing herself to be degraded, or was I an ancient parasite leeching sensation from the flesh of another? I began to get lost down the corridors of thought when I felt a sudden jolt. The giant above me had sensed my distraction and seemed angered. He now had a full, throbbing erection which he sank into my mouth. 'Suck this, you little bitch,' he said.

I was shocked. I felt a real blow to my sensitivity. I actually suffered indignation. This brute merely wanted satisfaction. He cared nothing for the niceties of the situation. And with these feelings another surge of lust ran through me. A deeper layer of fantasy-reality. I was actually being used. I was really being abused. I began to moan, and another popper went into my nostrils. Too much. I just opened my mouth and let him do what he wanted. He leaned forward and pinned my wrists to the mattress. And then he prodded the velvet head into every part of my mouth, up and down, sideways, around, poking at the very opening to the throat. I was able to take it partway, but the size of his cock staggered me. It must have been three inches wide. It seemed impossible to swallow such a thing.

Still he insisted, and soon I felt my throat gradually begin to open to him. A rush of drowsy agony filled all space. And at that moment I felt my legs being parted, and the great bulk of Tocco leaning on the bed. With no ceremony vaseline was slapped between my cheeks, and another cock thrust into my arse. The pain was excrutiating, for the move was sudden. I pulled my mouth back and whispered, 'Please, slowly!' He only shoved it in more quickly and rasped, 'Just spread your legs, whore!'

I fought for one final moment, and then succumbed. The cocks seemed to work in unison. My attention went from my arse to my mouth until I was nothing but the channel which connected these two sources of sensation. Images raced like fan blades through my mind, too fast to see clearly, but when even glimpsed, overpowering in their beauty. I was out into reality, fully, and my mind was reaping a harvest of conceptual flowers, so fragile that they might only be sniffed once and never known again.

Then sensation blotted everything out. As the cock penetrated deep into my throat, I gagged, and the gagging opened me clear down to the base of my spine, where Tocco was ramming in his prick with savage thrusts. For an eternity the three of us rose this blind wave of being, roaring separately in our lusts, and together forming a single organism performing its occult dance upon the bed.

And then the bubble burst. I could sustain the line no longer. I just wanted it to end. But they continued, and my self fell out while my body continued as a vehicle for their movement. I saw the entire scene as from afar, and watched myself with pity. Who was I? At that moment I was a body shot full of speed, high on poppers, lying in a strange room, having the tender tissues of my mouth and anus torn by two seemingly savage strangers, and enjoying it!

I began to feel dislocated and mad when, from a distance, I heard the voice of Tocco say, '. . . fantasy tension again . . . lost in rumination . . . give him another popper . . .' And the inhalator was thrust into my nose. Within seconds the magic happened again, and I relaxed. What did I care who I was, or what it meant, or who these people were? I was being fucked, I had a great prick in my mouth, and my body was aswarm with prickles of pleasure and pain. I was intensely alive. I opened wide to take it all in, gloriously, and immediately I remembered Susan in exactly the same position the day before. I was living out Susan's experience. The line, 'monkey see,

35

monkey do' began running through my head, an inane singsong.

I was her. She was me. There was no difference between us. And then I got the first glimmering of the lesson Tocco was to teach me that day. Realisation and sensation merged, and now I let it all hang out. I let all the last remnants of fear vanish, and offered my entire mouth and throat to the cock above me. And as soon as I did, the cock no longer seemed hard, but I could feel the softness of the skin and the texture of the serrations along the rim and the lean ripple of muscle inside. I grabbed my ankles so I could be fucked more fully. And the two of them, now moving as one, pumped their hot pricks and balls into my waiting sucking body, and as the throb of ejaculation sped into my arse and up into my stomach, the cock in my mouth let loose a tongueful of acrid, pungent, delicious sperm, which I swallowed and swallowed and swallowed until there was nothing left and I was gulping air.

After a while, the two of them disengaged and got off the bed. I lay there, utterly spent, stunned, spinning, rapturous. The doctor looked down at me for a long while. 'Very beautiful, Michael,' he said. 'You learned a good deal today, but just as important, you showed that you know how to fuck, really fuck. Not a mean achievement in these grey days of shallow accomplishments. Yet you are still a novice, and the early stages of learning are the most strenuous. We'll talk soon to integrate some of your experiences, but I think you deserve a treat right now.' He turned to Susan and the other man and said, 'Can the two of you do something nice for Michael?'

And as I lay there, the slim, very pretty young man licked gently and methodically on my cock, while Susan lifted her nurse's skirt and sat on my face, spreading her cunt lips with her fingers. She rubbed my mouth and tongue with her cunt by moving her pelvis around and down into me, and while I felt my cock begin to climb towards climax, Susan spent herself and filled my mouth with warm, spunky, white, viscious secretions.

Afterwards I immediately fell asleep, and I awoke happy and refreshed. I took a shower, dressed, and, feeling ravenously hungry, went out to see if I could find the communal dining room.

CHAPTER FOUR

After the meal I went out into the hall. I would have loved to have gone out for a walk to clear my head, and on an off chance tried the front door, but as I expected, it was locked. I turned and found Susan standing behind me. She motioned towards the door and said, 'I know it's frustrating at first, but in the city it's a necessary precaution. People do sometimes freak out, and it wouldn't do to have them running naked into the street.'

This was more like the Susan of the first day, and there was no trace of the irascible woman I had met in the hallway the night before. I wanted to make reference to it, but with her there so warm and inviting, what had happened twelve hours ago seemed unimportant. She took my hand and said, 'Come on, I want to show you my room.'

Her space was somewhat larger than mine, also without windows, and with evidence that she had been in it for a while. There were pictures and wall hangings, an expensive Persian rug on the floor, and all the other paraphernalia of daily life strewn about. I couldn't resist the temptation. 'What's a nice girl like you doing in a place like this?'

Whatever pale humour might have been in the remark was not even acknowledged. She looked at me with utter seriousness. 'Sit down, Michael,' she said. I flung myself

41

into an armchair, lit a cigarette, and waited. She seemed to be searching for the words. When she spoke, it was like cold fire. 'I like to get fucked,' she said. 'I like it all the time. In the cunt, in the arse, in the mouth. I like lying luxuriously on a bed with my legs spread wide, feeling a great big cock sliding in and out of me. I also like to go down on my knees in back alleys to suck off perfect strangers. I even enjoy rolling around a bathroom floor while half a dozen guys piss on me. I like to be whipped, I like to be humiliated. I like to have my cunt eaten out, I like to lick cunt. Anything that's got to do with the sexual sensation, I like. I'm a bitch in heat, all the time.'

'Are you a nymphomaniac?' I asked.

'No, nothing like that. It's not a compulsion, and I'm not frigid. I come like crazy. And when I get tired of sex, I go off by myself and lie on a beach for a month or so, and get in touch with who I am without my relation to anyone else. I'm just a woman, and like all women, I'm insatiable.'

'That's not been my experience.'

'Women are afraid. They don't know how to be animals. And then, even if they do discover themselves, its so hard to find a man who is really a man, not some image of what he thinks a man ought to be. I've had to wade through hundreds of creeps to find the one or two who really did it for me, who understood who I am and what I want. Oh, it was all right in the beginning, getting fucked by some clunkhead who stood so low on the evolutionary scale he was practically still breathing through gills. But you know, unless there is a shared consciousness, the experience becomes boring. I tried putting ads in the sex papers and got mostly misspelled obscenities for my trouble. Finally one of the letters sounded intriguing. It turned out to have been written by one of Doctor Tocco's assistants. I came here and went through some of the same changes you are now getting into, and the rest is recorded history.'

'How long have you been here?'

'About a year. I can't tell you how much I've learned and unlearned. Hip as I was, I had a list of prejudices a mile long. But Tocco is good. He's the best sexual philospher alive.'

She paused for a moment, then smiled. 'I'll get us something,' she said. She went into the next room, and I kicked off my shoes. I was becoming interested in the story and in the woman telling it. Up to now everything had been so brisk and strange that I had not noticed that the people here were actually quite warm and friendly, despite their quirks. For the first time I began to feel normal. This wasn't a madhouse after all. These were just intelligent people, intensely dedicated to finding out all the intricacies of sexuality. They had faults and probably made mistakes, but that was like people everywhere. I sank into a comfortable bin of sentimentality. Susan seemed like a thousand girls-next-door, only without the shame and pretence. She was an example of what a woman could be, and I had a staggering vision of a world in which every woman was as free as Susan, and every man as strong as Tocco. It would indeed be a race of giants.

She came back into the room, having changed into a white toga-like outfit that had long slits down the side. As she walked it became obvious that she had nothing on underneath. She carried a tray with Black Russians sparkling in icy glasses. 'Tocco doesn't usually like unsupervised liaisons,' she said, putting the tray down, 'but an occasional breather from "research" won't hurt anything.'

We sipped our drinks and smoked a bit, and she put some Scarlatti on the stereo. Our eyes said many things, and finally the words came. 'What were you doing before you came here?' she asked.

I sighed. 'It's really a long story which seems interesting in detail, but is really dull in synopsis. Basically, I'm an ex-fanatic. I've joined almost everything at one time or another, political parties, church groups, avant-garde artistic cliques, communes, drug scenes; I was even a guru chaser for a while. I held the usual run of jobs, from

43

dishwasher to high-priced do-nothing executive in a publishing house, getting by on personality and glib horseshit. But you know, running through it all was sex. Even though I didn't know it at the time, that was always the dominating passion, the unifying thread which gave me my deepest identity. And, like you, I got bored making it with people whose heads were as tight as a virgin's arsehole. And I willy-nilly made my way here to find . . .' And then I looked up. Susan was looking at me with warm moist eyes, a little smile at the corners of her mouth.

'Do you like the beach too?' she asked, slightly mocking.

Then, as though following a hidden signal, we were in one another's arms. Her body was very warm and soft. Everything we did was gentle and small. It was a different universe from what happened in the hallway the other day.

I reached into one of the openings of the gown and started to stroke her skin in gentle, undulating movements. It was less that I was caressing her, so much as discovering her for the first time. Learning about the texture, the curve, the friction, the moisture, the hair . . . using my fingers like eyes to taste the sensual reality of her body. And where I touched her, she responded with awareness of being touched. She did not need to move or cry out. I received all the messages through the aliveness of her skin.

Then there was no longer *her* and me, but the single phenomenon of sensation. I can't even say we shared our feelings, because that would imply two of us, and in this touching there was only one, a single living being involved in and conscious of its own ecstatic tone.

She reached up and slowly unbuttoned my shirt, and where the shirt fell open she put her lips. It was not the greedy sucking of the desperate, but the loving awareness of the awakened. We lay like that for a long time, easily undoing one another's clothing, basking in the fullness of one another's bodies, going from a tender distance to

44

sudden rushes of passion which would have us holding tightly and completely to one another.

Finally I reached down, and not losing contact with the flow between us, undid my pants. She also moved her hands and opened the clasps of her dress. And then we were naked. Now I had time to drink in her body slowly. Deep breasts that hung exposed in tender vulnerability. Nipples that had already begun to wrinkle and harden. Long expanses of smooth skin over evenly contoured skeleton. Her cunt was shaved clean and vaulted deep under a high pubic bone, like some great sea cave perpetually penetrated by the warm salt sea. She had full, very wide lips, and eyes whose keen intelligence was now suffused with clouds of longing.

It all came home to me at once, the brightness, the sexuality, the humour, the toughness, the tenderness, the beauty. Everything I had ever hoped for in a woman now lay in my arms and was moving towards me with wet openness and desire.

I ran my hand all over her. She turned and shifted to her side, and I explored her back, fingering the delicate curve of her spine, tracing one by one the vertebrae that went from her neck to the top of the deep cleft between her buttocks.

Her breathing was long and full and I placed one hand on either side of her rib cage, for a long moment doing nothing but feel the fragility of life with each breath as it surged in and out. I was exalted by an almost holy reverence for her body, for the very wonder and joy of it. I moved myself down until I was at eye level with the backs of her legs, and then ran my tongue up her thighs, licking and nibbling the entire expanse of flesh, moving in concentric patterns towards the inside and up to the treasure where her legs met. I could hear her gasps and moans of delight and felt her legs slowly, almost imperceptibly move apart. I looked up and could see the cunt slit unfolding as she opened up. With a long thrust I glided the flat of my tongue right up to the cleft where her cheeks rose up from her legs, and licked in a long arc

45

until I had buried my face completely in her arse. I smelled the aromoas rising from her cunt. She arched her back and brought her cunt close to my mouth, inviting me silently to taste the deepest part of her.

I was overcome with the lust and holiness of the moment and collapsed into her warmth. I heard her moan and she began to move, grinding her pelvis into my face, seeking for my tongue to get deeper and deeper into her. I was beyond all thought of technique. I tore into that immense small space and sucked and bit and groaned and lost all vestiges of any reality except the hot, wet gyrations of cunt and arse over my eyes and nose and mouth.

She pushed back and came up on her knees, so that the entire underneath of her hung open for anything I might want to do. She kept her shoulders low on the bed so that the angle of penetration would be the most acute. Fleetingly, amidst all the loved vibrations that swam through me, I appreciated the fact that she was so skilled that her body had its own sexual intelligence. I glued my mouth to the now-inflamed gash, my lower lip rubbing her clitoris, my tongue playing into the grainy section of cunt just past the actual opening. I drew a great long breath that seemed to last for an eternity, and then her entire vagina ballooned up and I felt a stronger suction drawing me in. It was as though she were sucking my entire being into her. I drew even harder and pulled the balloon of air back into my lungs, and then pushed it out again, full into her cunt. She went wild with passion. Her head swung crazily from side to side, her arse moved in jerky gyrations, her spine rippled like worms. For a moment an incredible tension hung in the now-immense pocket of vacuum that our mouth and cunt had become, and then she gasped. Her whole body went rigid as the inside of her cunt arched and formed a great still cavern. And then it broke, wave after wave of convulsion and sobbing; I drank and drank of her until the cycle ended, and we both slid forward and lay there, sated.

After a while, she stirred. I looked up at her and her eyes held a light I had never seen before in any woman.

46

She drew me up and kissed my mouth and face. 'This is for you, Michael, only for you. I have never let another man have just this before. Only you have this special part. This is just for you. Now, fuck me. Put your cock in me. Let me give you my cunt.'

Trembling, I pushed myself up and saw her lying on her back, her legs apart, her breasts quivering back on to themselves, her arse forming a cup on the sheets. 'Here, take it,' she whispered. 'It's all yours, it's just for you.'

My cock was almost bursting, and I lowered myself slowly into her. Immediately the heat and wet of her cunt changed the electricity of my entire body. Waves of relaxation washed over me, eddies of gratitude and joy. I felt my face light up with love. I was like a child overwhelmed with goodness. 'Oh, Susan . . . Susan . . .' was all I could say.

'Yes,' she hushed in my ear. 'Yes, baby, it's all us.'

And like that we fucked, cock and cunt becoming one organ, no separation between us, but just a single joyous riding through time into realms of timelessness. And our entire eternity was the smell and sound and taste and sight and touch and balance of the glorious, shitty, sublime human body. Deep, deep within we heard the call, the summons to climax. And a great heat and tumult began erupting throughout all existence, with our eyes locked to each other and our minds a single awareness, with jiggling breasts and heaving buttocks and drooling mouths and cries from some primeval plain, we came and we came and we came.

I must have lost consciousness, because I next remember waking up in Susan's arms and the sweat between our bodies had dried. 'Susan,' I called, and she gently opened her eyes. She smiled. 'Hello, darling,' she said. And in that instant fear struck. For there was no recognition in her gaze. And I wondered how many other times and with how many other men this had happened. It was not jealousy that bothered me now, but a sense of having been cheated somehow, of having been promised something unique, and receiving a beautiful present, but one which came out on a production line. Did she know who I was? What was in her mind? There was no way to ask without being clumsy.

She may have sensed something for she asked, 'Is something wrong?' 'No,' I lied, 'it's just that I was wondering about the time. Tocco said something about an experiment this evening.' With the mention of that name, I snapped out of my meantime nirvana and plunged into contextual reality. Still, this is one time I was glad he hadn't burst in with one of his bits of esoterica. 'Probably time for us to be getting dressed,' she said, and we climbed off the bed to get our clothes on.

On impulse I grabbed her arm and asked outright: 'Susan, while we were making it, what . . . I mean, were there any things in your head that . . .'

But she cut me off. 'It's too soon for us to go into that,' she said. 'Let us enjoy it as it was.'

'But what it was is what I want to find out about,' I protested.

She looked at me levelly. 'What more do you need to know?' she asked.

I realised that I had come down too heavily on the moment, and I backed off. 'No more than I now know,' I said.

She stepped quickly into my arms and put her head on my chest. 'Oh Michael, I know it's difficult, and it's going to get harder. And I don't want to sound like I know more than you, but it's just that when you've worked with Tocco for a year, you are able to see things, somehow . . . oh, I don't know how to explain. We had something very beautiful and special. Just hold on to that. Remember, no matter what else happens, or you think you see happening.'

My doubts melted and I held her close to me. Then she stepped back. 'We have to be going,' she said. I watched as she pulled her toga over her head, and saw her body disappear beneath the cloth. It is always sad when a beautiful woman puts her clothes on, but this time it was almost heartbreaking. I thought of what her body looked

like under the gown, and I felt another erection beginning. But it was one of those greed hard-ons that lead to
pinched orgasms, so I just let it subside. I dressed and
went to my room to put myself together before going
down to dinner.

CHAPTER FIVE

Dinner was like a family affair. I met Susan in the hallway upstairs and we entered together. I felt like a beau with his prom date. Our time in the room had roused romantic feelings in me which I knew were dangerous, but which I enjoyed too much to dispel.

The dining room now held about twelve people, including two girls, Sarah and Jean, and their mothers whose names were, I learned, Sylvia and Joan. These two latter were among the most fervent in the group, having been with Tocco for many years and willing to let their children experience, from birth, the widest possible range of sexual play. I flashed the Greek temples in which children were trained from a very early age in the arts of pleasure.

Again it was serve-yourself style, but most of the food had been cooked and a salad put together already. Halfway through the meal, Tocco picked up on a piece of random dialogue and began one of his expostulations. 'It shall be interesting to see,' he said, 'whether, after a thoroughly sexual childhood, these two enter into anything like a latency period. After all, the only way to find out whether latency is cultural or genetic is to test the variables. The problem of science to date is that it has been willing to create nuclear weapons and napalm to kill, torture and maim millions of men, women and children, and yet raises its puritanical skirts at a simple little experiment in the pleasure function of the young. If my experiments were found out, I would be prosecuted and jailed as a fiend and a monster, and yet the swine who make fortunes from implements of war are considered pillars of the community.' He paused for a moment, then went on. 'But let me not burden this company with my tirade. The congenital hypocrisy of society is not something you need to be convinced of.' And saying that, he looked directly at me and added, 'Or is it?'

I felt apprehension at his words but could find no proper reply. I fell back to my food and we finished the meal in silence. Just before dessert, Susan got up and excused herself. I asked her where she was going, and from across the way Sylvia teased, 'My, my, getting proprietary, aren't we?' Susan left without comment, and I had coffee and cigarettes in a dejected mood. Soon there were only Tocco and myself at the table. I looked up and saw him watching me with a look that seemed to hold a great deal of pity. He rose from the table and said, 'Well, Michael, are you ready to proceed with the evening's experiment? The difference with other times is that tonight you will be a spectator, with the hope that the distance will give you greater objectivity. It will take place in the basement.'

I followed him downstairs to a room which was some twenty feet square, furnished with an odd assortment of couches and chairs. Across one wall was a large movie screen. Facing the screen, on the opposite side, was a small raised platform with two steel-rimmed chairs. It was to the chairs that Tocco led me. But as soon as I had sat down, four men sprang as if from nowhere and held me while Tocco handcuffed my wrists and ankles to the steel tubing. I tried to resist, but Tocco said with a soft smile, 'Nothing shall be done to harm you, Michael; this is just in case you suffer a lapse from objectivity.'

I struggled with the anger and fear inside me, but I realised that there was nothing I could do. Also I believed

Tocco, that he meant me no physical harm. I resigned myself and settled into the seat, and began to wonder just what it was that would take place when the peripheral lighting went dim. A soft throbbing drum filled the room, and eight naked men came in and sat in a circle about ten feet in diameter. They gave off a powerful smell and vibration, with something of the jungle in the ferocity of their silence and purposefulness.

Then, from the shadows, a woman walked in. She was made up in bright gaudy lipstick, and was chewing gum. She had her hair done in a starched cone piled on her head. She wore a thin blouse which accentuated her breasts, and a skirt almost too tight to walk in. Her thighs and arse bulged out in an obscene invitation to plunder. The outfit was completed by three-inch spiked heels. She looked like a grotesque parody of the plasticised office secretary, a mindless bit of well-proportioned protoplasm.

I began to smile in anticipation of the scene; then I looked a bit closer and almost tore my skin attempting to leap out of the seat when I realised that the woman under that garish get-up was Susan!

I whirled my head around to Tocco, but he was unruffled. 'This is the fantasy, Michael, the one that Susan has chosen to work on tonight. It is an advanced exercise, and is being done mostly for her own sake. And your presence adds a nice touch, but try not to see it as a personal affair.'

'You're mad!' I rasped. 'You must know how I have begun to feel about Susan!'

'Precisely, Michael. And it is those feelings that you must come to terms with.' He turned away from me and looked out towards the others. 'Here we have the archetypal cockteaser, the woman who holds the favour of her burgeoning body in promise to all men and yet gives her favours to none. She is a tense, castrating bitch, and that is but a cover for a frightened teenage girl. She is walking home alone late one night. Suddenly she turns a corner and is grabbed and whisked into a room. Inside the room

55

are eight men who have had no sex for weeks. It's an interesting bit of drama, don't you think?'

I peered into the gloom. Half of the men were black, half white. Two had major deformities, missing arms or legs. Two were brutally ugly. I couldn't tell whether or not it was makeup that made them so. One had a cock that was some twelve inches long in its limp state. I turned back to Tocco. 'You can't subject her to this, Tocco! It's inhuman!' Tocco rumbled deep in his belly in an almost silent chuckle. 'I?' he said. 'Why, Michael, this is *her* fantasy. And you share in it.'

I was outraged. 'Me? I don't want to give . . .'

He interrupted. 'Don't you? Haven't you wanted to give a woman you were enjoying to other men? Let her be used by them? Let her be fucked by them? Haven't you? Come now, no dishonesty.'

'Yes, but . . .'

'But!' he thundered. 'But *you* wanted to set up the circumstances! You wanted it to meet the neat outline worked out in *your* mind! Reality is bigger than that. As you will find out. As you will find out in full!'

The power in his voice stunned me, and I slumped back in the chair. I looked to the centre of the room. The shadows had grown erotic. One of the men had set up a low murmur: 'Come on, baby, stick out your arse. Let's see those tits.' Others joined in: 'Hey baby, you want it in the mouth? Spread those legs, pig, give us some cunt.' Susan just stood there at first, and then one of the men reached out for her leg. She seemed genuinely frightened and pulled back. Another closed in on her. She tried to get away, but now there was no exit to the room. She was being backed towards a wall and she screamed at the top of her voice, but the room was soundproofed also, and no amount of noise she made could do any good. The voices continued, insinuating, gravely: 'You ain't gonna get out, not till you lick every cock in the room, not till you suck every one of us off, not till you spread those thighs and get fucked by every man sitting here. And you're gonna beg, you're gonna beg for it. 'Cause you want it, don't you? You really want it.'

As he spoke, I could see Susan's knees begin to get weak. She stood uncertainly against the wall and then began to totter out towards the centre, dazed. A silent scream formed in my mind. The men began to crawl towards her. She was transfixed, between wanting to escape and hypnotised by what was about to happen. Finally they were at her feet, and eight pairs of hands began moving up her legs, under her skirt, touching, pulling, pinching. She swayed back and forth and shuddered as though a sudden chill had entered the room. Her legs were being pulled apart, and the tight skirt formed ridges across the crotch and outlined the curves of her arse even more. Then, slowly, deliberately, she parted her legs. There was a long, long moment of tension, and then one hand went all the way up and closed hard on her cunt. She uttered a single cry, 'Oh God, yes!' and then sank down into the middle of them.

They pulled her flat to the ground and then went about their business quite deliberately. They laid her out spread-eagled and began removing her clothing. She closed her eyes and rolled her head from side to side, as though she were saying no, but at the same time her mouth opened and her tongue began working slowly. First her shoes came off, and then one reached under her skirt to remove her stockings. One man unbuttoned her blouse and the bra peeked out from the opening. Then two of them grabbed her skirt and slowly yanked it off her legs.

She lay there with just panties and bra, and seemed so small and helpless among the men that my heart broke. But with my pain ran a current of excitement that I could not suppress or hide. And it was not so much that I wanted to be one of the men down there, although that was true, but that I wanted to be Susan, lying vulnerable and ready to be plundered by anyone who came by. Then they closed in on her and just began to maul her, rubbing their hands all over her body, sitting on her, putting their cocks and arses on her, rubbing themselves into her.

They reached a point of near-frenzy when I thought they might begin tearing at her, but they stopped, and, again quite deliberately, began removing the rest of her clothing. The bra was unhooked and her soft white breasts tumbled out and quivered. I let out a low moan. Then two of the men grabbed her panties and dragged them down her thighs with excruciating slowness. I looked at her face and saw that it was frozen into a mask of expectant repugnance.

Then one of the men leaned down and began whispering in her ear. It was impossible to hear what he was saying but the effect on Susan was devastating. She began whimpering and crying. She whipped her head from side to side and kept moaning, 'No, no, no, no.' But another of the men came forward and slapped her hard across the face. She opened her eyes in shock and then slowly sat up. She took her wig off and her beautiful hair cascaded down her shoulders. Then she wiped her face with her skirt and took most of the makeup off. I saw the transformation take place.

Tocco leaned over and whispered *sotto voce*, 'You see, if she stayed completely in role, she could hide behind that. Now she has to face the fact that she, Susan, as she is, wants very much to have this happen to her, without any theatrical cover-up.'

I looked at her, and for a moment our eyes met. I can't describe what took place, but I had to look away. She was as beautiful and tender as she had been that afternoon. And then she lay back almost luxuriously, closed her eyes, reached down, and spread her tender cunt apart with her fingers.

At once they were all upon her, putting their fingers and hands into her cunt, reaching and digging between her legs, going into her arsehole, spreading her legs wider and wider. The man went back to saying things in her ear again, and again her face contracted in a strange kind of pain. But as she sobbed 'no' to him, she kicked up her legs, grabbed her ankles with her hands, and spread her legs as wide apart as they would go.

They swarmed over her like ants. For a moment she was almost lost from sight. And then some definite action began to emerge, as one after the other of them moved around to lick or bite or kiss different parts of her body. Hands and mouths plundered her box and her mouth and her breasts. At one point I saw that her cunt was already dripping wet and her nipples as hard as buttons. Then one man lay on his back and the rest of them lifted her up and lowered her on to him. His cock pointed straight up, and they manoeuvred her so that it came right to her arsehole, and then pushed her down. She fell back and gasped. She began clutching at the air with her fingers, but they pushed until she was completely impaled, and the hard cock was totally buried between her soft buttocks. Another then came from the front, delicately moved his cock from underneath and worked his way into her cunt. For a moment it seemed that she stopped breathing. It was as though she were possessed of some instantaneous over-whelming vision that froze her to the spot. Horror and ecstasy rippled through her in competing waves. Then a third man knelt by her shoulders and rammed his cock harshly into her open mouth. There was no movement for a second, and then everything happened at once.

Susan began gurgling deep in her throat and started twisting her pelvis back and forth, side to side. She wrapped her arms around the man on top of her and ran her hands over his shoulders and through his hair. She reached up and grabbed the cock in her mouth and caressed it tenderly. It was as though she had six arms, all moving at once, not knowing what to touch first. The other men swarmed in on her and grabbed her breasts and buttocks. The eighth man continued the patter of obscenities in her ear. I don't know how long they rode like that. I must have passed in and out of consciousness because at one point I remember having an erection, and at another feeling my thigh sticky with sperm. I had come, just watching.

One by one they pulled out and then looked at her lying there, and then began using her like a puppet. First

59

on her knees, where cock after cock was put in her mouth. each time she began listlessly and ended by gulping greedily. Then they put her on her stomach and each of them fucked her in the arse. Then they fucked her in the cunt. Position followed position, and the air was heavy with sweat and come.

When I thought they could do no more, they had her crawl on the floor after each man to lick his feet. They pulled back from her and she went after them. Grabbing their legs, rolling on her back and pulling their feet onto her, into her mouth and on to her breasts. One stuck his toes in her cunt. And she rolled, begging for more. They began to kick at her and spit down at her. At that she moaned ecstatically and opened her mouth wider. They brought their cocks close to her cunt and then pulled back, leaving her quivering. At one point she lay on her back, mouth open, pulling her cunt lips apart with her fingers, begging to be fucked, to be beaten, to have anything done to her that they wanted to do. The man with the immense cock, now swollen to outrageous proportions, flung himself on her. It didn't seem she could contain him, but he pushed in relentlessly, inch after inch, until he was three-quarters of the way in. A look of beatific joy spread over her face, and then he gripped her and plunged in to the hilt. She folded in the middle and grabbed on to him like a baby holding to its mother. And from her mouth came wails of the most indescribable terror and rapture, wave after wave of total sound gushing up from her innermost being. And he, snarling and tearing at her, slapped her face mercilessly and drove the immense cock into the farthest reaches of her cunt, splitting her with pleasure and pain. He came into her with a ramming, bucking movement, lay still for a moment, then pulled out.

Susan lay totally inert, totally open, probably even totally ready to give herself to be killed. And the man who had just fucked her walked up until he was standing over her chest and sent a long stream of yellow-green urine right into her mouth. She keened in ecstasy and swallowed it noisily. Then another squatted over her and lowered his arsehole onto her mouth. She reached up and pulled him further into her, and I could see her cheeks cave in with the suction. As though toying with a disgusting object, they came in turns and fucked her again, or had her suck them off, or peed on her, until they had come so many times that they were exhausted and she was caked with excretions.

Then, to my shock, the screen lit up, and on it came the figures of two people. I blinked twice, then saw that it was a film of Susan and myself, one that must have been made that afternoon from a secret recess in one of the walls in her room. It must have been shot with a telephoto lens, because every nuance of expression was caught close up, every whisper, every glance. I was dizzy with surprise, not knowing even which categories of understanding described what was now running through my emotions.

I saw a movement in the room and looked to see Susan crawling to the place in front of my chair. She lay on her back and raised her legs. Then she reached down and stroked herself between the thighs. She offered her cunt to me. Simultaneously my handcuffs were released. And the voice on the screen came up to full volume. It was Susan's voice, saying the things she had so lovingly whispered this afternoon: 'This is for you, Michael, only for you. I have never let another man have just this before. Only you have this special part. This is just for you. Now, fuck me. Put your cock in me. Let me give you my cunt.'

'Let me give you my cunt,' the Susan lying before me said, her voice a grating whisper. I looked from the warm, gentle Susan on the screen, to the ragged, filthy dreg of humanity leering up at me from the floor. Visions of betrayal and disgust flamed through me. And all the love I had in my heart rose up to clash head-on with all the hatred that filled my soul, and I shot up from the chair and loosed a cry so terrible, so complete, so final, that it burned every feeling my being had ever been capable of knowing.

I stood for a long moment and felt a cleansing deep pain which I knew had sealed forever the door to the kind of tenderness that I had always thought was a sign of love.

I felt a pang of great loss, and then closed the door on the myth for good. Tenderness was just another facet of personality, no better or worse than any other. My metatheatrical education was continuing on schedule.

I felt a stirring in my cock and saw that it was becoming erect. I looked down at Susan and felt . . . absolutely nothing. Everything for the instant had become pure perception. I opened my fly, walked off the platform, and smiling, plunged my cock deep into Susan's bruised cunt. The lesson had been driven home. Cunts are, first and foremost, for fucking. The rest is dramaturgy.

As she clasped me to her and began moving in that rhythm which I had already come to know so well, I heard the voice of Doctor Tocco, now thin and dry, as from a great distance, saying, 'Bravo, Michael! You have come a long way. But we are only now at the foot of the mountain.'

CHAPTER SIX

After fucking, I got up and left rather quickly. I felt drained of all interest in anything, and the only remedy was sleep, as a full, delicious tiredness soaked my body. It was a feeling of deep privacy and contentment, and for the first time in many years I made contact with a part of myself that seemed like home. My mind was empty, and if there is such a state as nirvana, I was in it at that moment, beyond all turmoil and struggle.

I stumbled into my room and barely had the energy to take my clothes off before flinging myself face down on the bed. For a few ecstatic minutes, I let the currents of tiredness run through me, and then I shifted a little, and fell into a black moving slumber.

It was an odd state, as though I were awake and asleep at the same time. I had no consciousness of any particular thing; it was more like a low-level awareness, as though the organism were humming to itself as all the life functions went on. I had a sense, or rather, there was a sense, of blood coursing through my veins and arteries; the great pump of my heart thudded slowly, and pinpoints of electricity flared up at nodal points in my nervous system.

And after a while the dreams began. They were not like dreams I ordinarily have, but seemed more like reality. Things appeared dimensionally and with weight.

Yet, everything had a spectral quality, as though the objects were transparent. It was an actual borderline feeling, as though fantasy and reality totally merged to produce some hybrid state which was neither fully one nor the other.

At first there were only vague shapes, and the sense was of an underwater scene. Greens and blues and purples coalesced and formed and dissolved. All things moved in a dance of quiet chaos. Then the shapes became sharper and the colours changed to brighter blue. Reds appeared. And, through it all, a quality of number came about. Not actual numbers, but the sense of thingness, of unity, of discrete entity. It was a silent music, a movement of law without any substance clinging to it. I felt totally calm and utterly isolated, as though I had landed, the sole human being, on an alien world which was not hostile to me, but simply had no way of relating to me at all. Ghosts of emotion fluttered through me, and I hovered between panic and bliss.

The most unnerving thing about the experience was that there was no sense of separation between myself and the dream. I was the dream and the dream was me. All reality was a single thing, and that thing was the movement which surged about in absent awareness of itself.

The colours darkened and changed to browns and blacks. And everything seemed to rise up and fold in upon itself. Then, without knowing how or why, I knew that this was the formation of a giant cunt. Simultaneously I was the cunt and inside the cunt and watching the cunt from afar. The sides were in constant motion, a steady rippling like the way tall grass flows in the afternoon wind. It was warm and moist, a kind of Hawaiian feeling of lassitude and ocean.

Suddenly shock waves ran through the atmosphere. There was a quickening of pulse and convulsions of the walls. A sweet tremor ran through everything, and the first drops of a pearly-white liquid began to ooze from all the folds. It was pure honey, a sweet, sticky delight of mouth-slackening fluid. Again a tremor ran through the air, and now the drops began to mingle together to form small rivulets. The atmosphere grew heavy and a deep musky smell emanated from inside the recesses of the cavern. From a great distance there was a low moaning sound and a rustle like the wings of a bird that have been suddenly disturbed. A feeling of imminence pervaded all.

Suddenly it seemed as though the skies opened, and a rush of white light flooded the opening. The cunt lips were parted. By now a kind of frenzy washed through everything. An urgency that throbbed like drums.

The lips parted wider, and a kaleidoscope of colour and sound sped into the hole. The deepest, most secret parts began to unfold and open themselves to the light. Simultaneously a great heat poured out from the pores of the walls, and from the black ends of the womb blasts of searing air rolled like tumbleweed throughout the cavern, and rushed out of the opening. The chaos grew, as movement and heat and wet churned together in a growing mix of near desperation. There was a feeling that something had to happen and soon.

Just then the cunt hole parted very wide, and the outer lips and inner lips peeled back. The cunning centre of the opening itself was exposed, tender, pink, ruffled. At that point all awareness trembled. Inside was all yearning and soft; outside was all demanding and hard. Then, in a stroke, a massive purple-rimmed engine nudged at the passageway.

Ripples of excitement seized the cuntly world, and the pulsating hole yielded slowly and lovingly as the round-rimmed cock nosed its way in. For a long, long time there was no sensation except each fraction of an inch of cock as it moved past the cunt opening. It seemed endless, as though the passage would endure forever. The opening stretched wider and wider, and as the tissues were pulled apart, spasms of joy shouted into the recesses of the cave.

The cock moved in ponderously and solemnly, its single eye seeing all at a glance. And then the dance began.

The cock pushed in until it had lodged itself as deeply

as the cunt could allow. The mood changed from anticipation to fullness. The inner walls waved and clutched and grasped the shaft in a hot, pulsing grip. Showers of fluid fell everywhere. The aroma was as deep and rich as black earth overturned in the spring. The cunt sang in exultation.

A movement of a different kind began. At first all the shaking was internal, rising up from below the surface of the skin. Then the flesh itself began to move. Ripples ran up and down the walls and massaged the cock with a thousand tiny gestures. Large movements began to grow in the deep places beyond where the cunt itself lay, and the shock of them reverberated throughout the canyon of frothing excitement which the cunt had become.

The cock responded with its own massive movements, and started rocking in and out, thrusting to the top, to the sides, to the bottom, deep into the inner recesses. Soon the cunt went slack, overpowered by the great machine moving inside it, and began almost gasping for breath, seizing the cock with great gulps, sucking at it, licking it, exploding bombs of heat into its flesh.

Now, almost as though a great bell had begun to ring, a new sense of imminence arose. A deep roaring sigh echoed down the corridors of the mighty cunt. And with one final roll, great tidal waves of unendurable pleasure broke and washed again and again through all the layers and folds and membranes and tissues of the now searing hot and violently convulsing cunt. And at that, the cock tore loose in throbbing spasms, shooting stream after stream of gushing balm all over the hungry and thirsty walls of the cavern.

A moment's blackness passed, and suddenly I found myself sitting bolt upright in bed, a cold sweat rimming my forehead. The dream hung in palpable reality before my eyes, and for an instant I was trapped in that insane state where I know what reality is, but cannot break the overpowering spell of the fantasy. My mind, which just a half hour ago had been so peaceful, now teemed with thoughts too fast and slippery for me even to ponder. It was like a mad tickertape machine, punching out speculations and concepts and fears. I felt violently sick and launched myself from the bed to go running into the toilet, where the remains of the evening's dinner splashed in grateful release from my stomach.

I sat for a long time, digging the cool of the tile floor, my head resting on the toilet seat rim. The vomiting had made me calmer and control returned, but a boundless sense of emptiness whistled through my soul. I got up slowly, threw some cold water on my face, and went into the bedroom. Sleep seemed out of the question for a while, so I turned on the light and picked up the only thing in the room to read, Tocco's pamphlet on the Institute for Sexual Metatheatre.

I flipped through the pages at random until a phrase caught my eye. It read: 'And so the individual comes to a point where it seems he must deny love itself, for that too is seen as merely another mask in the endless drama. Only then, if he successfully casts off, without bitterness, but simply and finally, all vestiges of his romantic mind, can he enter a land where he not only rediscovers love, but finds a way of loving that is so free, brave, and full, that he wonders how he lived so many years in that prison to which we can only give the name, Social Conscience.'

The words had a profoundly relaxing effect on me, and almost immediately I felt better. I lay back to think and found to my surprise that I was sleepy. I shut the light, and was about to drop again in slumber, when for no accountable reason I began sobbing like a child, in great gulping spasms, while hot tears rolled down my cheeks, and I cried out 'Susan, Susan' over and over again.

I cried for an hour, and finally, I slept.

CHAPTER SEVEN

The next day depression hung over me like fog. I woke up very early and went down to the kitchen before anyone else was stirring. I took a few bags of food and went straight back to my room and propped a chair under the door knob to keep myself private. I didn't want to see anyone during the entire day.

I made some instant coffee with hot water from the tap, and settled down with a cigarette to mull over what had happened. Clearly, the scene with Susan yesterday afternoon had been a set-up. It seemed she had lured me into fucking her just so that the film could be made and later used during the gang bang. I shuddered at the cold-bloodedness which such behaviour implied, and then almost immediately chided myself for the feeling. I had wanted to be in the big leagues; I had spent a good deal of my adult life railing against the hypocrisies with which men and women, men and men, and women and women belaboured each other. Intellectually I agreed with the tactics being practised on me, but the final vestiges of desire for a certain kind of intimacy died hard. Innocence had been lost, and there was no going back to it. All that was left was the struggle to come out the other side of experience.

It felt good to be sitting alone with my thoughts, and gradually a sense of balance was restored. The turmoil subsided and I felt a new surge of power beginning inside me. I knew I would not quit now. And with that thought, the memory of the night before came back, only this time I was able to savour fully its erotic content, and I felt my cock beginning to stir as I saw the picture of Susan's naked body lying in the middle of all those men. I wondered at my brief flash of identification with her, my wanting to be her at that moment. Although I had long ago realised that I was bisexual, I simply thought that meant an ability to enjoy male and female bodies indiscriminately. Generally, when I wanted to fuck, I found a woman, and when I wanted to be fucked, I sought out a man. The issue was more subtle than that, of course, and with women or men I played many roles. Never before had I so clearly understood my desire to *be* a woman, and for the first time I speculated on whether I might be a trans-sexual. Yet how to explain my clearly male delight in the female body, my enjoyment of my own erection, and my passion for cunt, a passion which reached such heights that often while fucking I could feel what was happening in my partner's cunt more than I could feel the sensations in my own cock? Some realisation nibbled at the corners of my mind, but I did not have the words to formulate it, to pin it down.

Just then there was a knock at the door. My first reaction was to ignore it, but I was seized by a perverse whim, and went over to take away the chair and open the door. I expected Tocco or Susan, but Joan, the mother of Jean, walked in. I was completely surprised. 'I just came by to say hello,' she said. 'Hello,' I answered, somewhat coldly. We stood there for a moment and then I motioned her in. I closed the door and went to sit in the easy chair. For a long moment she looked at me, then came over and knelt at my feet. 'Actually,' she said, 'I came to do more than say hello. I came for something special.' And she reached forward and pulled down the zipper on my pants.

By this time I was suspicious of everyone and I moved to stop her. She grabbed my hands and said, 'It's all right. This is something I want to do. And you can go right on drinking your coffee and smoking. It's your cock I want to be involved with, not you.' I looked into her eyes for any sign of duplicity but saw nothing but lust; her mouth seemed to glisten with desire. The old familiar tingling ran up and down the insides of my thighs, and I leaned back, waiting to see what would happen next.

I wondered at the honesty of the woman. There were many times when I just wanted to suck a cock or eat a cunt, and let the interaction be between me and it, not the person. There seemed to be some essential quality of sex in that attitude, and some words of Tocco's ran through my mind: 'There is no one meaning of sex. It is as changing, as mysterious, as obvious as life itself. What we are doing here is learning the steps of the dance so we can experience all of its moods and challenges and fears and glories without tripping over our own psychological feet.'

As I lapsed into a kind of reverie, my body became aware of the gentle, precise nibbling going on at the head of my cock. Joan was exploring the intimacy of tongue and penis, licking, kissing, pressing. With each touch she not only felt her own pleasure, but reverberated to the pleasure that coursed through me. And because I knew she wanted to do it, was doing it for no other reason than her own desire, I could relax completely. There was no need for me to perform, or feedback, or make sounds, or tense in any part of my body. I also knew that she would suck until I came, that her entire action was a work of art, a single complex unified gesture whose aim was the taste of sperm on her tongue. And so wave after wave of uninhibited pleasure swept through me. I was neither active nor passive: I simply was.

When she had worked over every bit of the head with her tongue, she pressed it between her lips and began making small smacking movements. I felt the blood rush through my cock and into the rim and inflame the entire shaft with heat.

Then she moved down and began licking the entire length of my cock. Her head made long graceful curves as

75

it moved up and down, and her rough tongue tingled the soft underbelly of the now stiff prick. She worked down to the base of it and licked at my balls, sending a jet of concentrated thrill into my bowels. She licked slowly at first and then furiously, taking the balls into her mouth and providing a thorough massage. She nosed down into the crevice between my buttocks, and gulping a little, ran her tongue down until she reached my anus, and then cautiously inserted just the tip of her tongue. I slid down in the chair to help her, but she had already moved back and up, sniffing and licking the tender junction between cock and thighs, and then back up the shaft to the blood-engorged head.

Losing no time, she moved forward and took the cock into her mouth in one gesture, pressing her tongue in counter-pressure from the inside as I moved down into the back of her mouth. At once the tip slipped past the opening to her throat and I felt her gag ever so slightly as she swallowed the entire length of me. By this time every muscle in my body had gone slack and I slouched deeper in the chair. Then, with a finger she must have prelubricated, she pushed easily and firmly into my arsehole. The sensation was overpowering. I understood the full existential impact of the saying, 'I don't know whether to shit or go blind.' She found the prostrate gland, and began gently prodding it, so that excitement came from inside and outside, until I was one great well of warmth and pulsation.

I looked down and saw her working with the utmost concentration and care, looking as though she were performing some holy rite. And then I realised that this must be some form of worship for her. Not that she was worshipping me or any nonsense like that, but that she was worshipping the *act*, the very fact of kneeling and drawing sperm from my body. I burned to know what went through her mind at that moment, but as I went to speak to her, I felt the come well up in me. I reached for her in gratitude, for the beauty of what she was doing, and with that I spurted out jet after jet of thick spunk on to her lapping tongue. She pushed her mouth forward and sucked hard, drawing the last drops out of my cock.

She stayed there for a long while, sporadically squeezing my cock and licking the residue from the tube. Then she put my cock back in my pants, closed the zipper, stood up, and licked her lips in a parody of a salacious cocksucker. I snapped myself out of my slouch and began to get up, but she motioned for me to stay seated. 'No, I don't walk to talk or anything,' she said. 'I just came to suck you off.' And with that she turned and walked out of the room. She stopped at the door, glanced back, and said, 'Bye. See you later.'

I wanted to call her back, but I realised that she knew her own mind too well for me to get her into the game I wanted to play right now. I had agreed to a blow job, and that is what I received. Perhaps I should have contracted for a half-hour conversation before I let her go down on me.

It was amusing and exasperating, and as I sat back down my mind began racing around the old familiar turf. What is sex, after all? There is the reproduction, and the mystery of birth. But what about all the rest of it? The pleasure? The role-playing? The variations? Is the sexual act itself symbolic of a higher truth? Or is truth simply a sublimation of the basic sexual drive? Perhaps sex, despite its intensity, was just like everything else: a complex, ill-understood, sometimes pleasurable, sometimes painful, reflex. It seemed at times that the whole problem was hopelessly muddled, and at other times crystal clear.

Something clicked in my mind and I backtracked. At which times was it crystal clear? I scanned my entire sexual history in a glance and saw the obvious. Sex was clear while I was in the middle of it. At that time there is no questioning, there is simply acting, whether the acting be confused with fantasies or not. Only afterwards did the difficult question arise. It would seem, then, that the only time to do research on sex was while one was actually doing it.

Without being aware, I had begun pacing. I walked up

and down the room and suddenly realised that I badly wanted to see Tocco. Forgetting my earlier resolve to stay shut in, I went out into the hallway and headed for his study. Boldly I opened the door and went in without knocking. To my chagrin, he sat there unruffled, as though he had been expecting me for some time.

He smiled grimly. 'I hadn't expected to see you today, Michael.'

'That's probably a lie,' I answered.

He made low *tsk-tsk* sounds with his tongue. 'Now, now, doubting the guru will get you nowhere.' He laughed. 'What brings you here in such agitation?'

'You know that as well as I do,' I said, 'but I don't want to go into what happened last night. I need to talk to you about something.'

'That's what I'm here for,' he said, with only a trace of sarcasm.

I pulled up a chair, losing all feelings of enmity in the excitement of the ideas. I spilled out all I had been thinking in the room this morning. He listened patiently, nodding from time to time, and after I finished, waited a few minutes before answering.

Finally, he said, 'Very good. But you stopped before the next question.'

'Which is?'

'Which is, how to keep awareness of action from interfering with the full flow of that action while it is taking place. You see, if you think about sex after it is over, you are examining a dead memory. But if you think about it while it is taking place, then you are splitting your attention and that ends in conflict and frustration. It is necessary to go beyond the stage of knowing that you know.'

'I understand the words,' I said, 'but they don't connect with anything vital inside me just now.'

He fixed me with a long stare. 'You are very bright and it is tempting to give you further verbal clues, but that would not be to your benefit. The only thing at this point is to keep working. It isn't easy, but it is not impossible,

78

either. Keep working, without becoming compulsive, and I will give you little pushes from time to time, or, as you saw last night, heavy jolts. And one day you will realise that you have known all along what it is you are yet to discover.'

'Tocco,' I said, 'are you sure you're not a refugee from a monastery?'

He chuckled. 'You seem to have recovered your good spirits, Michael. I had a little surprise for you which I wasn't going to give you for a few days, but I think you may be ready now.' He reached under his desk and seemed to be pressing a button.

Suddenly a side door to the office opened, and two huge men stepped out. They were dressed in black tights and black hoods. I looked at them and smiled. More costumes, I thought. Tocco barked at them, 'Enrico! Thomas! Take this fool to the dungeon!' I barely had time to be surprised, for they came at me with lightning speed, and they didn't look too friendly. I half rose from my chair and they roughly grabbed my arms. My reflex was to draw back, but one of them reached forward and gave me a sharp quick chop across the bridge of my nose. I saw stars explode before my eyes, and felt myself slumping forward. A blow landed on the back of my neck, and I slipped into unconsciousness.

When I came to I was naked and tied securely to a wooden post. My arms were bound with a thick rope behind me and my ankles were strapped with leather. My eyes cleared from the mist and Sylvia emerged, no longer looking like a schoolteacher. She was dressed in almost total stereotype: black leather pants with an exposed crotch that allowed her cunt to hang out, the pubic hair curling around the edges of the material; a black silk blouse, opened to her navel. Boots and gloves completed it. Her hair was swept back in a severe bun, and in one hand she carried what looked like a six-foot whip. My first response was that this was a joke, but one look into her opaque black eyes quickly convinced me otherwise.

79

She walked up to me, paused a moment, and spat full in my face. 'More than anything,' she said, 'you want to grovel at my feet. You want to lick my boots and have me grind your face into the ground. You want to suck out my arsehole and have me sit on your mouth while you lick my cunt. Then you would like to have me pee all over you.' To my chagrin, I found myself getting excited at her words. She looked at my erection with a grim smile. 'And past that, you want to rise up and throw me to the ground. You want to force my arse to the floor and pry me legs apart. And then you want everything hard about me to melt into a pleading puddle while you jam your large cock into my tender cunt. You want me to plead for mercy and finally to fling my legs around you and beg you to fuck me and fuck me. Isn't that so?'

I quickly calculated that she was on a peculiarly heavy trip, and considering my situation, the best thing to do was inject a note of normality. 'Look, Sylvia,' I said hurriedly, 'just the other morning when we were having breakfast . . .'

My sentence was cut short by a sharp slap across the mouth.

'Silence,' she snapped. 'I don't want any of that stupid patter. You are much too glib for my liking, and you need to learn a new reality. You understand that you are completely at my mercy . . . *completely*?' She looked at me very hard. 'Of course not. You have no inkling yet. So I shall have to teach you.'

With that, she stepped back, and began, slowly and methodically to whip me. The first slashes so shocked me that I didn't really feel the full pain of it. But by the fifth lash, fear gripped my limbs and tongues of fire seemed to be threading through my body. Again the whip fell. I looked down. Blood began to seep from the cuts. I tried to twist away, but the bonds were tied by experts. There was no escape. I looked up and saw Sylvia's face, now flushed with excitement. She was just beginning to get warmed up! The blows now fell faster and I found myself screaming, shouting for her to stop. I didn't believe it was actually happening, and foolishly I expected Tocco to step in at any moment and put an end to it. But there were no signs of that.

'Sylvia,' I pleaded, 'stop, please stop.' And the minute I said the words, a dam seemed to burst in me. Suddenly I was crying and begging, asking her to have mercy, to please stop whipping me. The pain had become an agony, and each time the whip landed I let out a high pitched scream. Panic overtook me. The reasoning part of my mind told me that this is how most people probably react, and it only fed the flames of her madness. For a moment I told myself to be brave, and then the whip hit again, cutting through already torn flesh. I started sobbing and my head fell forward on my chest. And then, almost miraculously, the whip stopped.

Sylvia came up to me, and I raised my head to look at her. Her eyes were shining wildly and her breast rose and fell with deep breaths. 'You are going through the necessary changes in reaction, Michael,' a voice said. It was Tocco, speaking from somewhere behind me. 'But Sylvia is a true master. She knows when her slave is merely in pain, and when he is really broken. She won't stop until you are totally in her power.'

I shouted, 'Fuck you, Tocco!' But my words just bounced off the walls.

Sylvia stepped back, and raised the whip again. 'God, no, please,' I begged. The leather snake whistled through the air and hit again, and then again. And something in me snapped. I didn't care what was expected of me, or what my inner voice said, or what images I was supposed to live up to. I just wanted the whip to stop. 'Please!' I sobbed, 'I'll do anything you say. Please stop!' I began mumbling incoherently. My brain was fogging over and my body was a sheet of pain.

Through the slashes, I heard her say, 'Not yet, Michael. You don't understand yet.' And hit me, again and again, I didn't know what she wanted and I tried desperately to think of some word or stratagem. But the whip was implacable. 'What do you want?' I screamed. And she answered, coolly, slightly out of breath: 'You will know when it happens.'

'I'll do anything, anything! Please, I don't know anymore. I don't know what to do. I'll do anything. Please!'

And the last thing I remember clearly was wondering whether this was sufficient to please her. What happened next goes past my ability to fit into any category. But it was as though some great beast, that had been so deeply caged inside me that I never even suspected its presence, was suddenly loosed. And I heard great throaty moans coming from my throat. I strained at my bonds and howled shamelessly. I felt urine spilling from my penis and my mouth frothed over with foam. I was surging out of all pores and openings, and suddenly the whip ceased to be an enemy. It was the whip that liberated me. It was the whip that opened me up. The thing that was now myself yelled for me, begging to be beaten. Sylvia was good, Sylvia was God! Each lash was a blessing that liberated me from the invisible bondage that had held me all my life. My hands and arms were tied, but for the first time, my soul was free. I left all fear behind. 'Hit me.' I sang and begged for the whip everywhere. I asked to be cut loose so she could slash at my arse. I wanted to be beaten about the mouth and to feel the sting of the lash across my cock and balls.

Suddenly, without knowing how, I found myself cut loose, and I fell forward. Now there was nothing between me and my liberator. I crawled painfully across the floor to her and found myself slobbering and grovelling at one of her boots. Licking the top of it wasn't enough. I forced myself to go lower, to lick the bottom of the boot, to lick it and swallow all the dirt that had been imbedded in the sole. And no longer was I being forced to. I wanted to. I wanted to be as low and dirty and snivelling and insignificant as I could get. If Sylvia would chain me to her door, I would lick the boots of everyone who came to see her. I would be her slave, utterly and longingly. In a giddy moment, visions of Christ danced above my head and the words 'The last shall be made first!' circled through me like an old ditty. I seemed to see it all clearly: only the total slave was totally free.

As I lay there, crushing my face into the very floor where she stood, the whip began slashing at my buttocks. I moaned and squirmed and spread my legs so she could hit me deeper. Then she pressed her boot onto my face and began grinding me down, cutting the flesh with the sharp edge of her heel, bruising my mouth, squashing me. At one point she stood with one foot on the back of my head, and forced me, open-mouthed to lick all the ground near where she stood.

Then, a confusion of bodies was upon me. I didn't know who they were, nor did I care. Sylvia reached down and grabbed my hair. She yanked my head up and slapped me a dozen times across the face. Then she brought my face up to her cunt, and a warm salty stream poured into my mouth. 'Drink it,' she rasped. And I gulped and swallowed, like a man who has been many weeks in the desert. When she finished, she made me lick her cunt clean, and then threw me down. 'He's yours,' I heard her say. And then I felt myself being pummelled and slapped. Cocks went into my arse, into my mouth. I don't know how many, or for how long it went on. More people came, and soon I was covered with urine and sperm.

And then there was silence. Very slowly I lifted up my head and saw that the room was empty, except for Sylvia, who was now lying on the ground, her legs spread and her cunt slit open, the pink lips mocking at me. From some unknown resource within me, a surge to titanic strength heaved me to my feet. I stumbled over to her ponderously as she lay there, smiling, and fingering her twat. The whip lay idly to one side. Suddenly I was Samson, blind but with my strength regained, and Delilah sat on her pillows, mocking me. What tore through me was rage and anger, but the energy grew so great as to leave all labels behind. I felt as though I could fight lions barehanded.

With that, I flung myself forward, and began striking at the woman who had brought me to this state. I hit her face and breasts and cunt. I slapped her and punched her.

I rammed my knee into her crotch. She never let out a sound, but a look of unearthly joy suffused her face. And the more that happened, the more violent I became.

Finally, I flung her back and lifted her legs high in the air, and then spread them apart until I thought I would rip all the tendons in her thighs. Pure naked cunt shouted at me and I pushed her legs back until her knees were at her ears, and then, without hesitation, I plunged my cock straight into her, pulling hair and tissue indiscriminately. She let out a single sound, and then I rammed home. It felt as though I had penetrated clear up to her throat. With super-human energy I lifted my entire body and again and again slammed into her, literally cracking her open, until I could feel her vibrating like a volcano about to erupt. A mountainous orgasm swelled in me, and I shot it into her with a savage scream, as shudder after shudder of uncontrollable spasm rocked her body and she came in a wild leg-kicking convulsion, with her nails dug deep into my back and her cunt opened so wide it almost stretched around my pubic bone.

We hung like that for a long while, then she fell back. All at once a wave of pain and fatigue washed over me, and I rolled over, already lapsing into unconsciousness. Then a shadow crossed my eyes and I opened them to see Tocco going over to Sylvia. He was helping her up. 'Sylvia, my dear girl, how happy I am for you. You achieved it.'

A pang of bitterness hit at me and I spoke through broken lips. 'Tocco, you bastard, you used me! You did this just to get the energy out of me for her orgasm!'

Tocco came over and leaned down. He looked genuinely solicitous. 'Don't be angry, Michael. I told you we would be assisting each other in our researches. Besides, think how much *you* learned this afternoon.'

The truth of his words mollified me, but I couldn't resist a final thrust. 'Add another item,' I said, beginning to go black again, 'in the catalogue of ultimate experiences.'

Tocco stared at me. 'If you fully understood what you said just now, there would be no need for any further work on your part.'

I started to reply, but then I passed out.

CHAPTER EIGHT

When I woke up, I heard birds singing. For a moment I thought there might be something wrong with my ears; then I opened my eyes to find myself in a large Victorian-style double bed. It was in a huge room, and one wall was a series of French doors which opened out onto a garden. The sun was shining, and far in the distance I could see mountains. As far as I could tell, I was in paradise.

Except when I tried to sit up, and then a sheet of flaming pain swept over my entire body. Immediately all the memories returned, and I fell back, perspiring. This must be the country place that Susan had mentioned. I wondered whether there would be barbed wire fences, and then I realised that something had changed in me. Tocco would have no fear of freakouts in the country because the only people who came here were those who had passed certain criteria. For here was where the 'real' work was done, and I momentarily shuddered to imagine what could possibly come next.

So far, however, nothing had happened that didn't have its own inner logic, and each event, no matter how gruelling, was enlightening. Although I seemed to know no more than I did a week ago, I felt somehow stronger, clearer. My mind was sharp and bright, although I wondered whether my body could take many more scenes like the one with Sylvia.

I began to drift off back to sleep, when the inner door opened and Tocco walked in. This time he wore a simple dressing gown, and carried a tray with orange juice, coffee, and cigarettes. He seemed to be the very soul of good humour.

He sat on the edge of the bed, put the tray on my lap, and smiled. 'Michael, I wonder if you realise how much of a fool you are?' I was startled. I hadn't expected invective. 'I don't mean to bring your spirits down, but merely to point out that you are yet incapable of distinguishing fact from fantasy.' I rolled my eyes back in my head. It was starting already. He saw the gesture and said, 'Excuse me, Michael. You're right, I should at least let you have breakfast first.' He helped me to sit up, and I took a long, thirsty gulp of freshly squeezed juice. I could feel my blood sugar rising almost immediately, and my outlook brightened. I finished the juice, and it wasn't until I had begun on the coffee and lit a cigarette that he continued.

'You may think it odd that I don't give you more time to recuperate, but you are in an especially receptive stage right now. Your mind is clear and your body incapable of producing too much tension. So I want to proceed without delay.' He paused a moment, then took a cigarette himself; it was the first time I had seen him smoke. 'Of course, you have no difficulty in obvious matters, like crossing the street, where you know that the cars whizzing past, although an illusion in the cosmic sense, can mangle your body on the physical plane. But in sex, where the fine line between so-called reality and so-called illusion is crucial, you are still like an infant on a see-saw, carried away by the exhilaration of the swinging.'

'Doctor Tocco,' I began patiently. 'I don't need to hear all this. That problem is precisely the reason I sought you out.'

He nodded. 'Indeed. But a definition, especially at this point, is necessary.'

'What happens at this point?' I asked.

'Ah!' he said, and clapped his hands twice. The door

opened again and in walked one of the men who had formed the party of eight around Susan that night. It was the one with the gigantic cock. I took a quick inventory of my physical condition and shuddered.

Tocco leaned forward and said, 'This will undoubtedly be painful for you, but nothing like what you have already gone through. And the rewards will more than compensate for that. Unless . . . you really don't want to.' He seemed genuine in his offer to allow me a cop-out, but almost despite myself, I felt excitement rising in my loins. 'All right,' I said, 'let's go ahead.'

The big man, whose name turned out to be Samuel, came over and rolled my on my stomach. The breakfast things were put aside and the sheets pulled down. I was in bandages from neck to coccyx, and only my buttocks and legs were exposed. Already the sexual stirring had begun to grow strong. I wriggled a bit, and Tocco said, 'How easily the supposed female in you comes out, doesn't it, Michael? You feel yourself vulnerable, desirable, luscious.' The words dripped with sensuality as he spoke. 'All right then, prepare yourself, for we are going to take this trip together.'

My legs were spread apart and oil rubbed gently all over my buttocks. Fingers ran up and down the crack between my cheeks and insinuated themselves into the hole. I was tight, and I flinched, but Samuel was experienced, and he retreated, only to move back in again and repeat the process, until I was totally relaxed. The finger moved in slowly and more deeply. I raised my arse slightly and he inserted a second finger. The stretch was delicious, and I went through a series of inner changes. One moment I was a badly whipped man letting a stranger shove his finger up his arse, and the next I was a beautiful and irresistible woman, drawing the male power to me through sheer magnetism.

'Tocco,' I said, 'the fantasies are incredibly divergent.'

He leaned towards my ears and whispered very softly, like a Tibetan monk giving final instructions to a novice on his first trip: 'Just a touch of yin and yang, Michael.

All life is a swing between the opposites. Only for you, the strongest poles are male and female. See if you can relax and enjoy the swing.' Then he inserted an inhalator in my nostril and the heady fumes of amyl nitrate filled my lungs. Almost at once my body flushed with sensation. I don't know what the physiology is, but what I felt was blood rushing to the skin area, and every pore, every hair follicle, was alive to touch, to the air, to the ethereal currents in the room, and, most pointedly, to the fingers now thrusting inside me.

I arched my back fully and raised my arse so the fingers would penetrate more deeply. I wanted them to pierce to the heart of me. I reached back and pulled my cheeks open. As from a distance, I could hear my breath come in harsh rasps.

Then Tocco's voice: 'You let yourself get swamped by the sensation this time. I am going to explain this as we go along. I don't want you to remember it, it's all being taped anyway. But let the meaning of the words sink in. If you will notice, there was the split between the two images of male and female. Now there is a split between image and sensation, and you got trapped in the sensation only. Here, try this.'

He helped a pipe to my mouth, and I clasped it between my teeth and took several deep inhalations. It seemed to be a highly potent distillation of hashish, and as I smoked, Samuel thrust into me all the way up to his knuckles. Within seconds, however, the sensations grew dimmer, and I could actually feel myself swinging back into fantasy. This time I sensed myself as a great ancient god, poised on all fours, immense in size, totally alive for eternity. I was very still, and watching over an ageless desert. And as I flexed my animal forms, Samuel moved down and inserted the tip of his cock into my anus.

There is no accurate way to describe what happened. It was as though the universe opened. I straightened and felt like a streak of lightning frozen at the instant of highest impact. I was all energy, all creation.

Again, however, Tocco began whispering in my ear.

'That's all very well, Michael, but you are still Michael, lying on a rumpled bed, semi-delirious with pain and dope, having a great cock shoved up your arse.'

'No!' I voiced involuntarily. 'I am Baal!'

'Hah!' he shouted, almost deafening me, and flipped me over. Startled, I lay on my back, and Samuel grabbed my legs and pushed them back. Once again the popper was shoved into my nose, and left there until I had inhaled all of it. Again I soared off, past caring who I was, or where. All I knew was the overwhelming sense of . . . ? The sense of . . . ?

There was no word.

I closed my eyes and lay back to let Samuel begin his terrible long entrance into me, when a great weight covered my face. For a second I was startled, and then I realised that it was Tocco sitting on me with his full weight. I began to suffocate and tried to escape, but there was no getting away. Mounds of soft flesh moved down on me inexorably. I yielded, and went wild. I began to lick and suck and gulp. I didn't know what I wanted. It was sheer frenzy exploding under the engulfing arse. And as I bent to reach for more, the huge cock began to drive into me.

I was certain that I would be split apart. The pain was excruciating. I screamed at the top of my lungs, but the cry was muffled. And the more I screamed, the more the weight bore down on me. I gasped for breath and each gasp filled my mouth with flesh and hair and the rough stinging taste of arsehole. And then I went under, like a man drowning. I gave up all hope and caring whether I breathed or not, and with that, the pain stopped, and I started to sink into a deep, deep sea of sensation and imagery.

I opened my legs and in a last embrace took in everything, all the pain and joy and yearning and loving and hating and being that it was possible to feel. And the cock just entered and entered. It went into places where I had always stopped in the past, where I had been afraid of being damaged. But now I welcomed it. I could feel

91

the bones at the bottom of the pelvis separating. I thought, 'My God, at last I am really being had.' Tears came to my eyes, for this is what I had always wanted, to be filled, to be completely filled. And as I thought that, Tocco moved up and then leaned forward and put his cock into my waiting mouth, my mouth that had been longing for just that sensation, just that contact. And I knew that this time I wouldn't gag, that I could allow him to plunge as deeply as he wanted. And he drove deep and far into my throat.

My throat filled with the foam of churning saliva; my arse went liquid and warm. I could feel my breast heat up and my bowels become loose. Another popper went into my nose, and my heart filled with gratitude. *Oh, thank you for understanding, for knowing, for not waiting until I had to use words to let be known what I wanted.* And as the drug took hold I sailed off into a place beyond all power of description. And as I went out, I saw, as though standing by the sidelines, the figures of Christ and Buddha and Einstein and da Vinci, each in a place where no human being had been, each equally far out, each totally different. I knew now that I was going somewhere no human guide could help me navigate.

The music of Beethoven crashed in my ears, and as the glorious strains of the *Gloria* from the *Missa Solemnis* rang out, I saw the single last outpost – a great Gothic castle at the edge of the void. There, Gurdjieff strode the walls with his great bald head and flowing moustache, wearing a perpetual scowl, carrying a single banner that said TERROR. He looked up as I flew past, a look of pity in his eyes, then he smiled and saluted with his hand. And I was free.

And somewhere in that freedom, I felt the great throbbing in my body, the pulsing of cock and heart and brain, the hot cascade of sperm, and the single realisation which sang like all the choirs of mankind combined in one shout. LIFE it rang, and LIFE. And then, just at the moment when the seed should have landed, when all of this should have come home to be planted, in a searing blinding insight of jagged pain, I felt the hollow emptiness within me where there should have been a womb waiting for its fertile egg.

'No!' I cried, and in pain bit my lip clear through.

A long time passed; Tocco got up and Samuel pulled his cock out. I lay there, breathing heavily. And then Tocco leaned over and put a cold compress on my mouth. There was a great weariness in his eyes. 'So, Michael,' he said, 'we have reached the centre, haven't we? You've found what you've been looking for, and learned that you can never have it.'

I looked at him in wonder. 'How did you know?' I asked.

He sighed; he lit two cigarettes and held one out to me. 'I'm afraid that it has been obvious since I first saw you. But that isn't saying too much for my powers of observation. This may bring you down, but your crying need for a womb and baby in your belly is almost universally widespread.' He got up and began to pace. 'Do you want to hear this now?' he said. I nodded yes.

'The history of the world since the advent of the patriarchy has been one long, bloody quest to fill some aching gap in man's make up, and we have tried with war, with art, with science, with phallic rockets to the moon, and still there is no satisfaction. It doesn't take too much intelligence to understand that what we have been looking for is something we can't have.'

'But that isn't the only quest,' I said, 'we are also looking for an escape from death.'

'The only escape from death is in the continuation of life. The ego dies, there is no way around that. But life itself can continue. And it is to our everlasting shame that we are too greedy to be content with the continuation of life simply, that we want to make it ourselves and rob women of their essential glory. Soon the scientists (and again he spat out the word) will be making babies in test tubes. And all meaning shall disappear from the species forever. We will have become sterile.'

'Am I homosexual?' I asked, puzzled by his words.

'Oh, you idiot, everyone is *at least* a homosexual! That has nothing to do with it.'

My head began spinning. I lay back and suddenly realised that I was trembling. We had gone from orgasm to discussion so quickly that I hadn't had a chance to savour what happened. Now I let go, and let myself feel the delicious afterthrob in my arsehole and the tang of sperm in my mouth. I began to stretch luxuriously, and yawned. For an instant I felt like a cat, then like a woman. Even my face melted into soft lines, and then the realisation struck me. I looked up.

Tocco was staring mercilessly into my eyes. 'No, Michael, it is too late for that now. You can become as soft as you like, but never will you be able to have the full fantasy of being a woman. You can pretend, but you know that you are not. You can dress up, and have empathy, or play out the roles you have been conditioned to play. But the seed of awareness grows in you now. From now on, whether you suck a cock or fuck a cunt, it will have to be as a man.'

I grew disgruntled. 'You make it sound like a John Wayne movie.'

'Oh, no,' he said, 'it's not that easy either. I am not talking about any image of man. But you will have to come to terms with what it actually means to be the male half of the species, and not have any notions of inferiority or superiority, but simply the ability to examine the issue. And you will have to do it on your own. There aren't many real men around to learn from.'

'Are you a man, Tocco?' I asked.

His face grew soft and he smiled. 'Michael, from where you are, you can't even begin to understand my sexual problems.' And for an instant his eyes opened and I looked to plunge deep into his soul. All I could glimpse was a sense of incredible height, and rumblings of a power far beyond my ken. Then the inner door closed, and he was simply Tocco again.

He put his hand on my knee. 'You must be tired now, and I will let you rest.' He turned to Samuel, but I interrupted. 'Uh – can Samuel stay?' The thought of having that cock in me again made me giddy.

Tocco smiled one of his rare Cheshire-cat grins and said, 'Why, that's entirely up to Samuel.'

Samuel and I looked at each other and I felt myself go weak again. No matter what the metaphysic was, I still wanted to be fucked, and I could tell the feeling was reciprocal. Besides, there was an almost full box of poppers by the bed, and I wanted to take it on my stomach this time.

Tocco put on his dressing gown and began to leave the room. At the door he turned and said, 'Be careful, Michael. Now that you have begun to understand the difference, the true difference, between the man and the woman in you, you can no longer take refuge in your fantasies of faggotry. You will be able to see through all that socially-conditioned nonsense. And you will be making real decisions from now on, whether your primary vehicle will be homosexuality or bisexuality or heterosexuality. But I have a suspicion that your synthesis is a bit more subtle than any of those, and you should tread delicately for a while. The more conscious you become, the more weight your actions carry. But for now, by all means, enjoy yourself.'

As Samuel lowered himself on to me and I put my legs around the backs of his thighs, I could see Tocco sailing out yelling a cheery 'Carry on' over his shoulder.

CHAPTER NINE

During the following week I walked in Tocco's garden of delights, letting my body heal, and thinking over everything that had happened. It was like a friendly village. From time to time I would see people I knew, but knew only through having shared some more or less bizarre sexual experience with them. Already, however, the notion of strangeness in sexual matters was leaving me. My prejudices were melting off very quickly, or so it seemed. Before coming to ISM, I had considered myself quite liberal, and was tolerant of all forms of sexual practices. But there still lurked in me feelings that some kinds of sex were more 'natural' than others. I was moving past that, and also past the notion of anything being all right between two consenting adults. It now seemed silly for adults to consent to anything unless they had the fullest awareness of what they were getting into.

I also noticed that, in moments of lying about, I no longer conjured up sexual fantasies in the way I used to. Part of me regretted the loss of the ability to sink so completely into unreality as to forget the actual universe. Yet what I gained more than made up for it. Even the sky and flowers and the faces of the people around me looked sharper, more alive.

For a while I pondered over my last experience, and wondered whether I should consider plastic surgery, actually having a cunt built in. The thought was thrilling and I pictured what life would be like as a woman, but the lesson had been driven home fully, and I knew that I would only become a mock-woman, a physiological mannequin whose barrenness laughed at the outward forms of sexuality. For the first time in my life, I seriously asked myself what it meant to be a man, to be a woman. So much of what is considered sexual difference is socially determined, and even the biological differences were largely a matter of hormones. There was something more, and to sum it up with the simple line that women had babies and men didn't seemed reductionist in the extreme. Yet there it was. As with everything in life, the solution to one mystery just opened new ones and the quest for understanding never ended.

Further, I was aware that whenever in the past I seemed to have latched on to a truth, it turned into its opposite, stuck its tongue out at me and left me shaken by the wayside. It appeared that I could know what was true, but that it disappeared the minute I tried to formulate it. In his pamphlet, Tocco had written, 'The damnable thing about reality is its total unwillingness to be defined by the limited faculties of man.'

Meanwhile little surprises cheered my days. One afternoon, as I turned a path in the woods, I came upon seven teenagers, three boys and four girls, bathing in a stream. They invited me to join them, but I pointed to my bandages and regretfully declined. I sat down to watch them, for they were exquisite. There was not the slightest pretence or hesitation about them, not the smallest ripple of concern or questioning. They enjoyed their bodies and made no metaphysical bones about it. Once again I regretted that I was born in a time and place where the intellect was, for some obscure reason, considered to be man's crowning achievement. Such a contention seemed pretentious in the face of the golden breasts and flashing buttocks dripping with water, the open eyes and laughing mouths. I felt a sensuality that was not yet sexuality, as the girls ran and splashed, their cunts opening and closing as they moved. The boys were magnificent, with firm and unmuscled bodies, full arses, and young cocks that seemed ready to drip with sperm.

It was a hot, murmuring day. When they had played in the stream a while, they came out and flung themselves on the grass. Their cries and shouts died down, and a heavy buzzing languor settled over everything. There was a growing sense of oneness, not of a mystical or other-wordly variety; but the stream, the trees, the birds, the achingly-blue sky, the white bodies, the grass . . . it was all a single, all a blend of complements which had no purpose but to perfect one another in the total picture. I began to feel drowsy and found myself sinking into the rich grass. The day seemed eternal, and images of ancient Greek scenes danced before my eyes.

I put my face close to the ground and saw that it was teeming with life. Ants and odd bugs and worms chugged about as in a busy city. My eyes grew heavy and it felt as though everything was moving. I blinked, and realised that there was actual movement, all around me and in the bodies which lay at a distance. The bodies were rolling ever so slightly, contracting and expanding, sending subtle messages to one another through breathing and tiny movements of the muscles. Suddenly I saw that the seven of them were not so much a group of individuals as a single organism. They rocked like that for a long time, and then the movements began to get larger. They rolled and kneeled and stood and lay down and rocked and shifted in a slow and purposeless dance. Or it seemed without purpose until the pattern emerged, and the pattern was unison. Gradually, wordlessly, without a jarring gesture, they were joined.

I don't know how long it took, but presently they looked like a single body. At a quick glance, it was all arms and legs and heads. But as I looked closer, I could discern interior details. In an intricate and seemingly spontaneous way, they had formed a perfect circle of contact. I sat up and rubbed my eyes, for it was almost unbelievable. The young vibrant bodies were totally joined. Cock went into cunt, tongue went into arse, breast went into hand. I was so dazzled by the grace and perfection that I lost all sense of the erotic.

Until they started to move in rhythm.

Then the spell snapped, and I saw the rippling boys and delicious girls fucking. I began to zoom in on details. Here a young and barely-covered cunt oozed a copious white flow into the mouth of a breathtakingly beautiful girl who swooned in tonguing pleasure between the full thighs. She herself was being fucked from behind by a swarthy boy. There a mouth fell open in ectasy, and first one cock, then another, entered it. Again two pairs of male hands ran up and down a thin girl's thighs, gently nudging her legs apart while a third with an immense cock first threatened, then teased, then sank into her up to the hilt as she let out a moan so wide that the trees rustled.

My vision blurred and the individual scenes blended and merged and parted again, and then there was a total groping with everyone simply licking and thrusting and grabbing and opening and wanting so badly it was heart-breaking to watch. It became a flow of gleaming cocks and gaping cunts and breasts jiggling, and mouths and thighs and expanses of flesh. For a split second I hallucin-ated and saw them as a giant cunt pulsating in the middle of the forest, and I almost rose up to go and fling myself into it.

And then they broke up into couples. One pair went into a glorious sixty-nine, he on top, his cock moving deep into her throat while her lips pouted and attempted to kiss his prick in that impossible position, as though she couldn't suck enough, and his tongue went again and again into her wet, now purple cunt lips, while her legs rose in the air and her bottom rocked to and fro on the grass. Another pair sat in the classic Tantric pose, he cross-legged, serene and strong, she a whirlpool of energy on his rod. She writhed and thrust herself down, and moved in a wild frenzy, pressing her breasts against him, her golden hair scintillating in the sunlight. Then all at once she became intensely quiet, and there was no external motion. But at the spot where they were joined, where her crotch cupped and covered his genitals, one could sense the private internal communication between cock and cunt, and all the activity that was needed went on in silent awareness. And the third boy simply put his girl on her knees and spread her wide from behind. From where I watched, I could almost look right into her hole, which shifted and pulsated as she moved her arse in anticipation. He crouched behind her, half standing, looking like a goat-god with his long hair and heavy haunches. His tool seemed to be straining to burst out of its own flesh. Then, without art or thought, he just bucked into her hard, almost knocking her forward. But she dug her hands into the turf and braced herself against his assault. He thrust forward again and again, his cock emerging each time wetter and more gnarled, filled with lust and fire. Then, in an instant, her knees left the ground and she hung suspended on her hands and feet, now having the spring tension in her knees to bring to the fray. And as he rammed into her she simultaneously bucked back and up so that she caught his cock from below and forced it to lodge in the deepest part of her.

I grew heady with watching and completely forgot that there was a fourth girl, until she came up from one side and sat down next to me. She seemed very wistful. I looked over at her and she produced a very faint smile. Suddenly I felt very old, a mere second-best. I saw myself as aged and cynical and spiritually impotent in the face of all that exuberant youth, and a great weight settled on my chest. I looked down and then lay back to watch the passing sky.

But she leaned over and looked into my eyes. In them I saw all the hope that the species is born with, the freshness, the joy, the urge to live fully. And suddenly I was crying, not only for myself, but for every man and woman who comes into the world fresh and whole, and then is beaten down, year by year, until he or she becomes a suspicious, tired, hateful parody of what a human being can be. Anger flared in me, and I cursed all the bosses

103

and generals and presidents and parents and priests who so lose their sense of wonder and freedom that they must in turn destroy the love in their children. And then I saw that I couldn't even blame them, for they too were once young and alive, and they too are the products of some almost alien system which seems totally geared to destruction of the human race.

And like many before me, I groaned, and asked myself 'Why?' Why did it have to be that, of all the animals, we alone turn ourselves into slaves, we alone torture and jail our own kind, we alone are afraid of freedom? In a flash I saw all history, and realised that as long as men have been writing things down, there have been those who have tried, who have preached and taught, attempting to lift this burden from our backs. And always the same thing happened. Churches grew, or political parties were formed, or philosophies were expounded, and mankind merely exchanged one form of tyranny for another. And now, except for the infants this second being born, there is hardly anyone left, hardly a human being not crippled by this great emotional plague that sweeps into every heart and mind. War and pestilence hang over the earth like dark birds, the air is poisoned and the waters are filled with scum, and even mother's milk is unsafe to drink.

And as I wept, the beautiful angel in front of me, not knowing what was wrong, not knowing how to deal with it, did the only thing she could think of to stop my unhappiness. She lay down, took out my cock, and put it in her young sensitive mouth.

I looked down at her, at the smooth white body, at the gentle buttocks, at her legs bent at the knees so that her calves went straight up into the air, and watched her full lips curve around my cock. And while I lay there filled with anguish and hatred, while I cursed the foul thing that mankind had become, while I felt like a source of poison fouling everything around me, I let jet after jet of thick sperm spill into the gulping mouth.

She remained there for a moment, and I was filled with an overpowering sense of shame, shame which came out of some still vital sense in me that could not allow sex to come into my deeper feelings. Then she leaned over and spat the sperm on to the grass.

I was horrified. She looked up, and staring straight into my eyes, she wiped her mouth with the back of her hand. Then, with a look of scorn, she got up and walked away. I looked after her, unable to move. Too many unexpecteds had rushed too quickly into my world for me to assimilate them. Was this some trick? Was this another supposed lesson? I looked for Tocco but the glade was empty. What had gone on between the girl and myself? Had she used me in the same way, or had she picked up on my feeling of shame and reacted with a rejection?

Suddenly, with all the thoughts still unresolved, I found myself on my feet. Without really knowing why, I began running in the direction she had taken. I went into the woods and immediately everything grew silent, rich with that thick stillness that happens among trees. I stopped and then began again, walking gingerly this time. A thrill of expectation ran through me. I strained my ears and could make out the sound of her walking. The thought of her nakedness alone in the forest fired my sensibilities. I crouched and began moving swiftly in the direction of the sound.

Within a minute I saw her, and with a burst of speed I overtook her. She heard me coming and turned. A look of shock went into her eyes. Without losing stride I went up and slapped her full across the face. She gasped and went to her knees. My entire rational mind was screaming at me to stop, but greater forces were at work in me. I grabbed her hair and forced her face to my crotch. 'Open the zipper with your teeth,' I said. She trembled, then obeyed. 'Take that cock out with your tongue.' She reached in and worked my cock out. 'Now suck it.' She began licking at it tentatively and I shook her by the hair. 'I said *suck!*' She sobbed and then, with a gasp, she fell on it, taking the entire limp shaft into her mouth. She worked at it with her tongue from inside, and I felt it go hard. She tried to pull back, but I kept her glued close to the crotch, my pubic hair pushing into her face. The cock expanded inside her mouth, and having nowhere else to go, forced itself into her throat.

After a minute, I yanked her head back and flung her on the ground. 'Spread your legs,' I ordered. She opened her legs. 'Pull your cunt open.' She reached down and with four fingers of each hand, pulled the cunt lips apart. I fell on her, put my cock at the very edge of her cunt. 'Now look me in the eye,' I said.

She looked deep into my eyes and her gaze was hard, steady, spiteful. I slowly put my cock into her cunt. Just a little, then a little more. Her eyes twitched inside, and she fought to steady them. I pushed in a bit more, and her focus went hazy. She struggled to regain a sharp glance, and I lowered myself all the way into her soft and now moist cunt. Her eyes glazed over and turned in on themselves.

'Now,' I whispered in her ear, 'open it up.'

She opened her legs and my hips sank forward. As she continued to tilt her legs, my cock went deeper into her. 'Open it inside,' I said, 'open up your cunt all the way. I want to get all the way inside.'

And then I could feel it letting go: the unconscious tension, so habitual she didn't even know it was there until it was pointed out to her. And I sank past the cervix and lodged right at the mouth of her womb. And then I began to move. I covered every inch of her cunt. I moved in all directions possible. I went in like a starving dog ravaging a bag of meat. I went in sailing until there was no resistance left, and when she was totally open, I whispered in her ear, 'Give me your cunt. Make it mine.'

Then there was wildness. With a moan she let everything go. The teenage girl suddenly turned into a woman, and as she moved in deep frenzied circles, I grabbed her young firm arse and pushed her into me, rocking her back and forth, using her body like a giant hand. Her knees went to her chest and she put her feet on my hips. I lunged forward into the deepest angle possible, and her legs flew apart. I felt the bottom of my stomach drop and

I rode with her without reserve. She rose to meet me, and together we felt towards orgasm. She filled with liquid and ran over with heat. Her young cunt now lay lush and throbbing. And without warning she bucked and cried out, and came with her arms thrown tight around my shoulders and her legs trembling in the air.

We lay there for a moment. My cock still burned with the undelivered sperm. I was at the edge of coming, but it was sinking back into the shaft in that shrinking, painful retreat, so sickeningly familiar. I pulled out and rolled her over. Her arse lay before me, tempting and succulent. The crack was wet with secretions, and in an instant I had pried the cheeks apart. Her tiny anus lay exposed, bunched and flushed with deep red colours. I leaned forward and put the tip of my prick at the opening. She didn't move at all. Without hesitation, I leaned forward and let the weight of my body drive the cock into her arse. I looked down and saw the shaft disappear between the buttocks. She was tight, but without tension, so I slipped in easily and firmly.

I sat up and pulled her back towards me, so that she was half raised on her knees. My hands went down and pulled the cheeks apart, and I watched the tempting sight of her arsehole stretched fully around the thick base of my cock. I moved back and forth slowly, and revelled in seeing the tender flesh contract and give as my cock drew out and then sank deep into her. She began to moan, and I felt the heat rising in my balls. It was so delicious that I wanted to prolong it, but nature had heard too strong a call. So I let go and began to ride her arse hard and deep. She cried out, but at the same time pulled her knees together so that her arse came higher and fuller on to my cock. I reached forward and grabbed on luscious breast with my right hand and put the fingers of the other in her mouth. And squeezing her full round breast and feeling her tongue sucking and licking at my fingers, I jammed my cock into her anus again and again until a hot rush tore loose from my bowels and shot deep into her hole.

She immediately sank forward and I fell on top of her.

I lay there for a while, and when my cock was soft, I pulled out slowly and toppled over. The wood was silent and the sun was streaming through the tree tops. I closed my eyes and felt the peacefulness of the moment. And when I opened them again, Tocco was leaning over me. I felt so good I didn't even mind, and I smiled. If the girl had been sent as a game, I seemed to have won all the points.

Tocco chuckled. 'So, Michael. One short week after coming to terms with your manhood, the first thing you do is rape an innocent young girl. You may have a fine mind, but your behaviour remains, I am sorry to say, stereotyped.'

I thought I knew him too well to take that kind of badgering seriously.

'Listen, Tocco,' I said looking up at him, 'that girl is as involved as I am.' I turned to look at her but found that she was gone, silently and without any indication that she had ever been there. I began to feel uneasy.

'Fucking her was not what I was referring to. It is the intent that is important.' I began to protest, when I heard a rustling sound, and saw four men step out from behind the trees. They walked over and stood over me. 'In these parts,' said Tocco, 'the penalty for rape is death.'

I sat up, half expecting him to smile, and then I remembered the whipping and Susan's gang bang, and I realised that he might stop at nothing to carry on his research. Still, he wouldn't do that to a friend.

I was still thinking that as I was hustled to my feet and led towards the house with my four guards watching me very closely.

CHAPTER TEN

I was led into one of the rooms at the back of the house. It had nothing in it but a bed, and seemed to be little used. I was made to undress, and was then tied to the bed with silk cords. I tried to fight back, but was quickly discouraged by the bulk and efficiency of my captors. I wondered just what was in store, when a door opened, and Tocco entered, leading the seven young people I had just seen down at the stream.

They gathered round me like biology students looking at a specimen. Tocco, of course, assumed the role of professor. He cleared his throat and began in a very pedantic manner: 'The subject you see before you is at the stage where he is incapable of distinguishing between his want and another's need. We are not to blame for this, for like the rest of us, he is the product of his conditioning, and stumbles about blindly, harming himself and others in a confused, conflicted round of experience he pathetically refers to as "living". At your ages, you have not yet come to terms with certain problems; and Michael here is struggling with things that you will never have to face. This is the legacy one generation leaves for the next. You will have your own difficulties, however, so there is no unfairness in the process.

'Today, basically, we are going to explore, through his eyes, as it were, the question of selflessness in pleasure and pain. For Michael it will be a crucial bit of learning; but we can all benefit from what takes place.' He turned to two of the girls and motioned them towards me. 'Connie and Sydney, please, would you begin?'

The girls moved to either side of the bed and began slowly taking their clothes off. This was something totally outside what I had been expecting, and I didn't know where to look first. I had seen them nude earlier, but at a distance and outdoors. This was more intimate and dusky, and the act of undressing in itself was highly stimulating.

I decided to concentrate on Connie. My mind raced towards all kinds of speculations and fears, but there was nothing I could do, and hard experience had taught me not to try to outguess Tocco. The best thing seemed just to enjoy it, whatever it would be. Connie wore a simple dress which she began to pull up very slowly, past her thighs, over her crotch. And I could see her cunt hair, dark and matted under the flimsy panties she wore. I began to get hard. She pulled it higher until her belly was exposed; it moved in soft, shadowy ripples, making her navel pout in and out. I strained against my bonds to get closer to her, but it was futile. Then she threw the entire dress off, and her breasts stood taut and firm inside the brassiere. She was very full and deep-breasted, and her tits rose and fell as she breathed. She reached behind and undid the strap; the bra just fell forward, unlocking two lush jiggling melons of flesh capped by very small red nipples. Then she reached down and slowly pulled the panties off.

My helplessness in the face of her enticing strip infuriated me. She saw my state, and when she straightened up, she opened her legs slightly and pushed her cunt towards my mouth. She inserted a finger deep into the hole and moved it around, plunging in and out of the moist box, thrusting her pelvis back and forth in a fucking motion.

Just then I heard a sound and turned to see Sydney bending over to present me with a full view of her arse. The cheeks spread apart and her tiny arsehole peeped into view, and under it the brown frizzled hair around her cunt showed between her thighs. She put both hands under her buttocks and pulled her cunt open for me to see. I was thrashing with desire.

As though on signal, the two of them moved in on me. Connie crawled up on the bed and straddled my thighs. She ran her fingers down my belly, past my pulsing cock, and cupped my balls. I tried to lift myself towards her, but had no leverage. She did it for me, grabbing me under the arse and pulling me up towards her. Then she came forward, legs apart, and lowered herself right on to my cock. I let out a sigh as I sank into the young tight cunt. I didn't have a moment to enjoy it before Sydney knelt at my side and leaned forward to drop one of her creamy tits into my mouth. I reached up to suck it, and she pulled back, only to come down again, teasing me with its nearness. I felt as though an electric current ran through me. Sydney came all the way forward and filled my waiting mouth with her hard nipple and soft round breast, while Connie twisted and thrust on my cock, her cunt rippling inside, working like an incredibly sensitive hand, squeezing and pulling. I bucked under her, and rammed my cock up into her, again and again, until my arsehole tightened and I shot spasm after spasm into the eager cunt.

It was immediately unsatisfactory. My inability to move my limbs, and my initial surprise at the situation, had caused a tension which gripped my stomach and buttocks as I came, and I fell back feeling that slightly sour taste when I come, without losing all reservations. Connie moved away, and immediately one of the boys was on her, while another took Sydney from behind. Connie's cunt, already wet and filled with sperm, made sloshing sounds as the prick thrust under her arse and into the gaping hold. Sydney knelt on the edge of the bed so that the man behind her could take her standing up. They fucked with the same vigour that they had shown on the grass, and soon the whole room smelled of cunt juices and come.

Connie leaned back on to the cock at her behind, and brought her face down to cup my cock in her open mouth. For a few minutes I was out of it, not being able to get up again so soon. But the sight of the lascivious pleasure around me and the gentle insistence of the tongue around the rim of my cock soon roused me again. I raised one of those maddening seven-eighths erections, and another girl came in to add her mouth to the job. I raised my head to look down and saw that they were now stretched out full length, touching thighs and bellies and breasts. Their hands moved down between one another's legs, and a gentle rubbing of clitorises began. They started to moan and grind against each other, and their mouths now no longer concentrated on my cock. Rather, they were kissing one another passionately, thursting their tongues into each other's mouth, and my cock simply stood between them, receiving the benefit of the caresses they gave to each other. The excitement in me reached fever proprotions as their heads bobbed and pressed towards each other, and as their mutual heat grew greater, the ministrations to my cock grew fuller and richer. They came to a point of climax, and as they spent wildly on to each other's hand and fingers, they flung their mouths totally on to the head of my cock, which flared and called yet another orgasm from my balls.

With the pleasure this time came a pinch of pain resulting from the strain of coming again so soon after the first time, and as the sperm spurted out and into the air and spilled down on to their lips, I fell back exhausted. After a moment, everyone got off the bed, and they all resumed their watch over me. I began to feel frightened for, although it seemed that I was not to be physically harmed, I felt I was being herded towards something unpleasant. I also felt a dull ache in my testicles, and my bandages began to burn and itch.

Tocco resumed his talk. 'So far, the subject is behaving well. Let's wait five minutes and continue. Everyone take a break.'

From what followed, it was clear that it wasn't to be a

coffee break. Like athletes in their prime who love to train, the seven of them began another round of sexual gymnastics. They played a series of short games, with changing couples attempting to outdo each other in far-out sexual postures. The prize went to a young man and girl who fucked with him in a total head-stand, the girl wrapped around him, her legs grasping his waist and her hands holding his feet. They did fine as long as they remained still, but when she tried to roll her pelvis, she threw him off balance and both of them came tumbling to the ground, to the applause and cheers of the others.

My interest was largely academic at first, then I began to feel still more stirrings. The sight of so many exuberant cunts and stiff cocks at once and so near was overpowering. Tocco clapped his hands; they stopped their games and began to close in on me. This time there was nothing specific, just a swarming of bodies. I was totally covered by flesh. Every inch of me was soon rubbed by cunts and arses and cocks and mouths and breasts. They seemed to form a gigantic fleshy chamber, and my entire body was the shaft it enclosed. I felt the throbs of energy rushing through me, and without my being fully aware of when, my cock was hard again. I was sure I couldn't come again so soon, but I had underestimated the power of numbers. With so many different ways and directions of touching, I grew more and more sensitive until, at one point, someone lowered their arse on to the stiff prick. I squirmed in painful delight, but there was no getting away. The buttocks rose and fell, and I felt the tip of my cock rub into the cheeks and into the hole and penetrate deeply into the tight warmth inside, and then begin the journey out, only to have it repeated again. Whoever was on top of me moved with practised ease, until the arse received its desired treasure, and I spurted still another jet of sperm into it.

This time it was almost entirely without pleasure and simply shot out in a burning spasm. The buttocks pulled away immediately, and my cock flopped back between my legs, sore and limp. The others disengaged and once more

I lay on the bed alone, feeling filled with disgust and fatigue. But I had hardly a moment to rest before one of the boys came forward with a tube of vaseline. He reached down and smeared it between my buttocks. It was the last thing I wanted. The thongs around my ankles were loosened and I could move my legs, but only just enough, I soon learned, to allow him to slip his cock underneath and take me in the arse.

Ordinarily it would have been very exciting to be fucked while tied down, having a number of people watch. Arse-fucking between men is an entirely different experience from that between a man and a woman. Perhaps it's because, having a cunt, a woman treats her anus as peripheral to her central pleasure. But for a man, it's the only cunt he has, so he cultivates its pleasures, learns to experience it fully. There is a further psycholgical factor. Fucking a woman always raises the problem of her having an orgasm, and there is a double tension going on. But when a man gets fucked, there is no strong question of coming. So he can relax.

The young man pulled my legs up at the knees and leaned in towards me. I felt his cock slip into the crack between my cheeks and probe at the hole itself. I tried to lock myself against him, but he had the leverage. Slowly his cock found its objective and pushed into me, inch by hard-fought inch. I found a perverse pleasure in resisting him, and the more I fought, the more my excitement grew. Then, suddenly, to my own amazement, I stopped the struggle and just opened up to let him have me. The cock entered deeply, and involuntarily I moaned. He found the vulnerable spot right under the prostate gland, and probed it gently. A warm glow spread inside me, and as he moved, I felt still another delivery of sperm bubbling towards the surface. My whole body protested, but there was nothing for it. And as he fucked me, my still limp cock dribbled out a few watery drops on to my belly.

He pulled out suddenly and harshly, and I gasped at the quickness. My eyes were stinging and my head spun, and I wondered what it was they were trying to do. What did this have to do with rape and the death penalty? The words danced in my head until the reversal came clear. It was I who was being raped now, and the execution was being carried out by fucking. I hung between horror and hilarity for a moment, and then rested in the knowledge that there was a physiological limit to what could be drawn out of me.

But I had not counted on Tocco's thoroughness. One of the girls came forward carrying a syringe, and barely had it touched my arm than I knew that a full dosage of speed would be coursing through my veins, forcing me to heights beyond my normal tolerance. I shouted to Tocco: 'This is unfair! You can't use drugs like this!'

He pursed his lips. 'Nonsense, Michael! Drugs are merely a means to enable us to get beyond what we would ordinarily endure. We pay a price for the intensity, but we return with nuggets of knowledge otherwise unobtainable.' The needle entered and I felt the liquid being squeezed into the vein. He continued, as the first rushes coursed through me: 'Have a pleasant journey.'

With that he motioned to one of the boys, who repeated the actions of his predecessor. The familiar weakness gripped me, and I sank into the melting sensations of giving. Once again a cock pushed into my anus, and this time I could feel it in intimate detail, the round rim of the head, and the expanding width of the shaft as it entered up to its base. I was too enervated to respond, but that didn't seem to matter. He moved with clockwork regularity. I lay back and let it happen. Without my being aware of its approach, another cock came into my mouth. And then a wet warmth covered my prick as I began to be sucked off yet another time.

Their erections seemed made of steel, with no promise of yielding. I prayed for them to come, but I realized that was not the objective. Soon I lost all sense even of sensation, and the fucking became a numb rubbing, back and forth, back and forth until it was totally unpleasant. I thought I was beyond caring, but still they fucked, and I began to be sore. My mouth felt like an open wound, and

117

my arsehole seemed to be torn and scratched. I strained against my bonds and the weight of their bodies, trying to make them stop, but there was no escape. Finally I tore my mouth loose and shouted. 'No more, no more!'

Miraculously they stopped, got up, and stood away from the bed. 'Michael is tired of cock,' said Tocco. 'Let's give him some more cunt.' To my own surprise, I found myself yelling 'No' to the very thing I had spent my life pursuing. But the girls came over and clambered on to the bed. 'Give him some poppers,' said Tocco in an oily voice. The inhalator was thrust into my nostril. It was a tribute to my state of exhaustion that I barely felt any effect.

Then I was smothered in cunt. Two of the girls climbed up and sat facing each other, their cunts touching and both over my mouth. But by this time what had been a sensual musky smell had become rancid. I felt myself gag, as both cunts and arseholes jockeyed to press into my mouth. The other two went to work on my cock, which was almost without sensation but, incredibly, hard. They rode on me for what seemed an eternity, changing positions so that cunt after cunt impaled itself on my cock and then joined the line which came to force itself between my lips. They kept putting inhalators in my nostrils until I began coughing and came close to passing out. Then the boys joined in and once again I was awash in flesh, but this time they tore at me savagely, biting me all over, thrusting into my anus and mouth, spitting, pinching. At one point a finger went deep inside me and began massaging the prostate again; I screamed in agony, but there was no relief. The finger kept working until I felt a searing jolt of pain and the sperm ran out once more and dribbled into my pubic hair.

To my horror, I began to sob. I felt like a piece of rotten meat with ants crawling over it. I stank with dried secretions, and every inch of my flesh ached. The cocks and cunts which had seemed so beautiful were now ugly, hurtful things, hateful and disgusting. I knew I could bear no more, when a warm wet sensation around my lips

118

convinced me otherwise. They were kneelng around me, squatting on me, and from their sex, thick streams of urine splashed on my body.

They finished, and wiped their cocks and cunts on my mouth and chest. And then Tocco leaned over, his mouth filled with bits of cheese and onions and hard-boiled eggs, and pressing his lips to mine, forced his tongue into my mouth. I gagged and retched. 'What's the matter, Michael?' he asked, 'don't you want a little kiss?'

He stepped back and clapped his hands. The door opened, and suddenly the room filled with dozens of naked people, old and young, beautiful and brutal. They filled the floors and walls. They began to perform obscene dances, shouting a stream of disgusting suggestions. They exposed their cunts and cocks and arses. They licked the air with their tongues.

My mind reeled, and I fled to the edge of a precipice where sex would never seem good again, where it would be permanently burned into my brain as something hideous. Tocco's voice boomed out, 'Here it is, Michael. The human body. The human farce. Do you want to get laid? Take any number of them you want, any sex any size.' He leaned forward and slashed my bonds loose with a razor. 'Sexual paradise on earth,' he roared. 'It's all yours!'

Part of me realised that this entire scene was just another lesson, and that I had to remain objective. But I was overcome by the ugliness that had been perpetrated. The sexual apparatus and the sexual act suddenly seemed a mindless groaning and slavering, a stupid sucking and licking, an endless thrusting and struggle. A war. The war between the sexes and among the sexes. There was nothing but slimy secretion and sheer idiocy. It all welled up in me, the fatigue and disgust and emptiness, and right in the middle of the academy, I threw up on the bed.

A rough hand grabbed my neck and thrust my face into the vomit. 'Lick it up,' said Tocco's voice. I retched. 'Lick it!' I gagged. 'No!' I said. 'You can kill me. I won't do that. I won't.' The hand rubbed my face back and forth in the vomit several times and let me fall.

As I lay there, covered with sperm and cunt juice and urine and vomit, sick at heart and confused in mind, Tocco's voice drifted down! 'The next time you feel like a *man*, and want to rape a young girl to show her how sterling you are, or the next time you lie in a woman's arms and compliment yourself on what a great lover you are, remember this. Spent, puking, fucked out.'

'I wouldn't eat the vomit,' I sobbed. 'I wouldn't eat it!'

There was a long pause. Tocco spoke slowly and reflectively. 'That's true. That's something. It's a very small thing to go on, but at least there's something to build a foundation. Now go clean up, and don't let me see you for a few days. Big man.'

I opened my eyes and found myself staring into Susan's eyes. Her face screwed up in utter disdain, and she coolly and calmly spit right into my face. And then turned and walked out of the room.

Suddenly everyone released me, and I fell back. I waited for what would happen next, but there was silence, and when I looked, everyone was filing out. In a moment, the room was empty. And I sat, in the deepest and fullest despair I have ever known in my life, robbed of the one thing that had remained the single passion that made living worthwhile. Tocco had destroyed sex, and there seemed nothing left.

CHAPTER ELEVEN

It took me a very long time to leave the room. All the spirit had drained out of me, and there was absolutely nothing I wanted to do. Or, to be more accurate, there was no one I wanted to see. It seemed that I had fallen into a very deep pit, and there was no way out. The present was intolerable, and yet I could not find anything in the past to cheer me, and the future stretched before me like a great bleak highway leading nowhere.

I was beyond all emotions such as self-pity or even despair. There was simply emptiness and I knew fully that no one could fill the void in myself but myself. I realised now that all my contacts with people in the past had had a sexual undertone to them, that no matter whether I was on the make or not, the thing that brought people alive was the sexual energy which ran through them. It didn't matter whether they were young or old, thin or fat. They had potential for ecstasy, and it was to that potential that I addressed myself. In my less ego-infested moments, I seemed to be able to bring out the sexiness in everyone, and so brighten the lives of people who had forgotten what profundity lay very close to them, right between their own legs. When I was on ego trips, of course, I played sexual guru, a role I blushed to think about now that I had seen a real guru in action.

I wondered whether I should ever find the spark again,

and even in the wondering, I realised that at that moment I didn't care. I was beaten to the core.

Finally I dragged myself off the bed and stumbled to my room. I went to the bathroom and took a long look at myself in the mirror. The face that stared back seemed scarred and devoid of life. For a long time I peered at myself, and decided that I had come to the end of the road. I shook myself to break the spell, and began the painful business of peeling the bandages off. I looked down and examined my body, covered with caked urine and scarred by Sylvia's whip. I couldn't believe that this was the same person who, just two weeks ago, had bounded into the brownstone with such arrogance and optimism.

I showered, flinching as the soap bit into the cuts, shampooed my hair, and shaved. There was something marvellously therapeutic in washing off the day's accumulation, as though I were ridding myself of all the harm that had collected during the experience. Clean, I rubbed oil over my entire body, and when it had been absorbed by my skin, I put on a pair of clean pyjamas, and dived between the sheets of the soft double bed to sink immediately into a deep, dreamless sleep.

For a week I kept pretty much to myself. It was out of no special motivation, just that I had no real interest in saying anything. My mind was beautifully clear of thoughts, and the weather and the scenery combined to restore a certain glow of health. If nothing else, I needed to come down from the heavy drug scene that had been part of the sex encounters. I walked in the woods, carefully staying away from the stream, and spent hours watching clouds sail by. In a very passive way, I was not unhappy.

But, by the middle of the second week, I felt a change. It was, at first, no more than a quickening, a gathering of pulse. I noticed that I looked at things more sharply, and I didn't avoid other people as much. And when, after dinner one night, I caught myself looking at Joan's arse as she walked past, I realised that the sexual juices were running again. The fact brought a quiet joy and a sense of panic. For I couldn't begin to even think about fucking someone without the whole scene of that afternoon spilling into my head.

That night I lay in bed with sleep far away. I was staring at the ceiling, watching the shadows thrown by the candle next to my bed. Absent-mindedly, I reached down and put my fingers around my cock. There was nothing immediately erotic about it, just the general kind of playing around that men do, which has been referred to on occasion as 'pocket billiards'. One of the things I had always liked about the gay world was that with the sexual tension gone, I had no need to feel embarrassed about tooling around in the presence of others. The action seemed to be basically a kind of self-reassurance, a putting of one's hand on one's manhood.

This time, as I fingered and stretched my cock, the mildly pleasant sensation very slowly began to change itself into an actual tingling, and for the first time in ten days I felt the first faint sexual stirrings in my loins. It might have been a cause for rejoicing and getting up to find someone to play with, but a heavy lethargy overcame me, and it was far more enjoyable to just lie there and feel myself.

My cock stirred and then began to swell. I felt its hardening, but as though from afar, and when I grasped it full in my hand there was no conscious intent to do anything.

Gently I began pulling the skin back and forth, and my cock now swelled quickly and in a moment lay fully hard in my hand. I massaged it and rubbed back and forth, feeling the hardness grow even more firm, until it stood like an iron rod filled with juice sensate, and throbbing gently. I moved my hand up and lightly rubbed the head. Pinpoints of flashing sensation ran through it, and I began stroking the entire length of the cock, from base to tip, in easy rhythmic motion. The head grew violet in colour and the warm pleasure eddies began to extend into my thighs and belly. I moved my hand faster and then, with a start, realised that I was highly aroused.

I raised up on one elbow and looked down. I saw the fully erect cock twitching with readiness. And yet I had no desire to fuck or be even vaguely involved with anyone else right then. I stared at the member with fresh eyes, as though I had never seen it before. It was a beautiful thing, majestically tapered, veined with blue lines running its entire length, jutting up from a tangle of curly black pubic hair and sloped up to the head, which flared out in a serated rim, now darkly purple. The head itself, soft and velvety, was superb in its curve and texture, and led to the slightly open mouth of the cock where, miraculously, both sperm and urine flowed. The old Latin phrase came to mind, that we are born between shit and piss, and I wondered at nature's aims in putting the source of our life and the pipeline of elimination in a single functioning member.

It seemed that I had never understood things so clearly, and then I realised that there was not a single fantasy in my head, not one concept or theory to muddle me. There was simply the fact of the thing itself. How many hundreds of times had I stuck that cock into arseholes and cunts and mouths, and never really sensed the richness and fullness of the action? Because I had never really seen my cock so simply before.

Suddenly the separation ended, the viewpoint which had me thinking in terms of 'me' and 'my cock.' *Me* was everything about me, my body, my talk, my thoughts, my emotions, my ideas. The cock was not a separate entity, to live its own life irrespective of what the rest of me needed and wanted. And yet, for so many years, it was the cock that, like a divining rod, led me to dig into things that I might not have otherwise bothered with. It was both a curse and a blessing, for it simultaneously opened worlds that no other part of me could get into, and for that very reason closed off worlds that other parts of me were starved for.

I lay back again and went inside my body; that is, I felt

myself as a single organism, an entity, a unit. And I felt not with just my mind, but with each bit of me, that every part was totally related to every other part, and that as I stroked myself now, it was not my hands doing something to my cock, but hands and cock in a relationship together. And what hands and cock did affected everything else, the rate of my heartbeat and the speed of the blood in my veins and the thoughts in my head and the way my skin felt. I was an entire orchestra, and I had to play in harmony or lose the chance to be a total human being.

I let myself slide into the awareness of my body as my hands and cock continued their dance. The fingers stroked lightly along the bottom of the shaft and twirled around the head. I drew my knees up and felt my head begin to roll from side to side. As the stroking continued, more of me went into motion. My pelvis began a slow undulating beat, thrusting up and back. I felt my face flush and my ears grow hot. I ran my other hand down and it began massaging my stomach, poking into the navel, coming up to pinch the nipples, and then running down again to cup my buttocks, and finally to run one finger into the arsehole.

Now I was moving quickly. Ripples of pleasure sent my legs to trembling, and I felt my spine begin to shoot energy from the coccyx to my neck and back down again. I heard sounds and then realised that it was myself moaning. I began to go into a tailspin, when all the lessons I had learned so far asserted themselves, and I let the growing concentration disperse, in order to allow myself to stay in a state of pure attention, so that I remained conscious of everything else; of where I was, and the shadows on the ceiling, and the fact of Being. At all levels of consciousness, I was awake. And in that state I could see the structure of my mind in perfect clarity, where the fantasies come from, how the thoughts are formed. And seeing all that, I was instantaneously free of it.

Now there was only the act, and without a flicker of tension, without a distortion of intellect, without a cramping of the feelings in my emotional centre, I let my body

127

ride its ride. My legs braced against the bed, my pelvis gyrating in its own rhythm, my hand curled around my cock and stroking up and down, my chest rising and falling with sharp breaths, my mouth slack and emitting sounds, my head thrown back, and unifying it all, my cock in growing heat and excitement.

Then I felt a turmoil in my bowels, and all of a sudden it felt like the bottom fell out. My arsehole opened and the walls inside rippled to discharge my finger. The heat tingled and began to rise as wave after wave of sheer energy rolled through me. It was immense and went far beyond pain and pleasure. It was the actual energy of the universe shooting through me.

My body grew huge with the charge that was building, and I felt a great reservoir of force building in my belly. It grew greater and greater, until no more could be contained, and then a long, slow, mighty eruption began. It flowed from every cell of my body, from every pore. It rushed through my entire frame, moving in gathering speed and intensity towards a single spot. It came together in the pit of me, somewhere just below the navel and deep inside, and then spun around on itself and plunged into my balls, which churned and then released all the sperm accumulated there. It boiled up my cock in scalding layers, and as my entire body rolled in spasms my pelvis broke into easy undulating thrusts, and the sperm spurted out in jet after jet for a long, long time, until it was all spent and lay in drops and rivulets across my chest and stomach.

For a long time I hovered in that space, and then sank back with a large sigh, a deep peace already beginning to pervade my body. Although I was already lying full on the mattress, the feeling of sinking into it continued, and I closed my eyes and seemed to be falling a great distance, falling and floating through space. I let myself go and plunged into myself, finding a great void, a featureless universe of movement with objects, of law without manifestation, of feeling without person. And for a brief instant, the single absolute true understanding of the condition of existence flashed in my mind, and I lost consciousness.

That night no one in the entire world could have slept more perfectly than I. But when I woke up in the morning, a profound sense of depression had already seized me.

CHAPTER TWELVE

As the day progressed, my mood grew worse. However, there was a difference from depressions I had suffered in the past. This time, I was strangely content within it. There was no sense of conflict, no feeling that I ought to be feeling something else. In my acceptance of how I was, I found a peace that was astonishing. I simply let myself go with the emotions and thoughts and sensations, not judging them, or condemning them, or making plans on the basis of them. I felt not a little like a character in a play whose script called for depression at this particular time in the action. And so the heaviness became no more or less important than the sunshine streaming in through the windows.

I lay in bed for a long while, and then, with no purpose in mind, got up and dressed and went out for a walk. It was a clear spring day, trees very green and vibrant and the constant dance of birds winging through the air. Without changing, my mood lightened, and although I felt totally friendless, without any understanding of myself or my problems, and with no one to turn to, I felt a release in the very fact of my poverty. I stood in the middle of a small grove and came to terms with the universe. Deeply and suddenly I ceased struggling. Everything was clear, and in a flash I realised that there would always be ugliness and pain, as there would always be truth and joy; there would always be the moment of total communion between one human being and another, and there would always be times of betrayal. And yet, somehow, if I simply stopped attempting to figure it out, trying to change it, but accepted the gift of my life with all its hardship and confusion as well as its beauty and elation, then never again need I feel that terrible sense of having been cheated, of wanting more, of insisting that things must be other than they are. And in that realisation, everything was better, without having become at all different.

My reflex was immediately to do something with this new understanding, but there was nothing to do. I realised that I had lost that urgency, that sense of quest. I was myself, totally and inexorably. No Tocco or sexual institute could change me because . . . and the insight came with the strength of thunder . . . because the change had already occurred. Somewhere, somehow, a mutation had gone on inside me, and although not a whit of my entire personality was different, I was utterly transformed.

It was at this point that I heard a noise, or felt a presence, and looked up to see Tocco standing by my side. He was barefoot and wore only a great white loincloth. His body gleamed with oil. And on his face was an expression of total openness and warmth. It seemed that I was seeing him for the first time, not as a guru or an insane fat man, but simply as a human being, filled with beauty and love, with great sorrow, and heavy with the understanding in his heart. I felt myself grow warm, and pure simple love poured out of me and washed over him. He smiled and his eyes shone, and for a long moment we remained like that.

I started to speak, but Tocco held up one hand. 'The details of what you are feeling are unimportant, Michael. I know where you are, and it's good to be here with you.'

I wanted to respond but no words came. He saw my impulse, reached down one hand, and helped me to my feet. We stood there, and he said, 'Now, there's something I want to show you. And there is only one thing I want to say about what you are feeling, just some words to plant in your awareness and let them grow.' He paused and turned as if to indicate the fact of our being there and said, 'It is obvious.'

I waited a long moment for him to continue, and then gradually realised that that was the entire message. I looked back at him but he just smiled a kind of cat-who-ate-the–canary grin and said, 'Come, let's take a little tour.'

We went back into the house and into Tocco's study. We walked straight through to a door which he opened to reveal an elevator. We entered, and then began to descend for a space I couldn't calculate, and stepped out into a hallway which ran in three directions from where we stood. On the right was a sign which said: 'Vuvu'; to the right another sign read 'Exit'; and the centre sign had written on it 'Corridor of Ultimate Experiences.' Tocco set out straight ahead and said, 'We go this way.'

The hallway was longer than I could see to the end of, and on each side were a series of doors. We went past the first of them, and each had a placard on it which read, 'Ultimate experience: Fetishism', or, 'Ultimate Experience: Transvestism.' I soon saw that behind these doors was a representation of each of the so-called perversions of mankind. Tocco began speaking. 'In this hall are the people who have gone through all the preliminary adjustments to their understanding of sex, and are now single-heartedly exploring the variations within individual forms. Once one understands fully that there is no such thing as an unnatural act, then any act can become an area of study, and through understanding it, one understands all.'

'How do they come to choose their . . . uh, speciality?' I asked.

'It's a matter of temperament mostly. Of course, there are interdisciplinary seminars, and the work-day is limited. After-hours even the researchers like to blow off steam.' He paused and turned to me. 'Where would you like to begin?'

I looked at the nearest door on my right and saw the

sign, 'Exhibitionist-Voyeurist'. 'That looks a good a place as any,' I said.

We entered the room and an astonishing sight met my eyes. Scores of men and women lay and stood and knelt around in odd poses, some alone, some fucking in groups, while others peered from behind chairs or through tiny binoculars. Although there were the usual sexual sounds, the room held an unusual silence reminding me, incongruously, of a library.

I scanned the room and my eyes fell on a young woman who couldn't have been more than twenty. She had long silky blonde hair, and wore an open blouse and slacks, which she would pull slowly down past her waist and over her buttocks as though she were undressing. But when she had pulled her pants down to her knees and bent over to accentuate a full, lush-lobed arse, she pulled them up again. I watched her for a minute, and when she caught my eye she repeated her act while staring unblinkingly at me. She looked down and I followed her line of sight to those inviting sweet buttocks, and then looked back at her to see her mouth the words, 'Don't I have a beautiful arse?' I shuddered and felt a thrill of excitement go through me.

Tocco whispered in my ear, 'She wouldn't let you fuck her, but if you wanted to, she would let you worship her, or, more precisely, her backside. You would have to learn to navigate the waters of her narcissism, to kneel to her arse, to lick it, to murmur into it.' But I was already doing something else, a kind of long-distance Tantric yoga, my body moving in almost imperceptible gestures to complement her dance. She picked up on it and for a while we just kind of leaned into one another with subtle vibrations, and without touching her, I was able to fuck her in the arse in a dozen different ways, knowing that she felt it, and was playing back with complementary movements.

Then a flicker caught my eye, and I wheeled around to see a giant video screen come alive with a picture of a cunt which formed the total image. It stood twelve feet high by eight feet wide, and must have been shot with a

136

close-up lens, because every fold, every hair, every glisten of secretion stood out in giant relief. Then fingers came into view, and slowly, very slowly, pulled the lips apart, and layer after layer of cunt opened endlessly, until the very bud centre lay exposed, pink, and pulsating slightly. One finger went to the heart of it and inserted itself, no more than an eighth of an inch. But with such magnification, it was possible to see the core of the cunt opening and sucking at the finger like a child's mouth at a nipple filled with milk. The finger tip went back and forth in the tiniest of movements, and rolled gently around, slightly expanding the grasping cunt hole.

I wondered why, when such exquisite grace was possible with such small movement, did we spend so much time grunting and crashing into one another? It seemed that in fucking we get carried away by the mounting energy, and lose sensitivity control. And as with any other interactive machine, the less sensitivity there is the more signal input there has to be, and in our case that amounted to adding on more bodies, more drugs, more whips, more of everything, until one was glutted. But when the sensitivity increased, one could do less until, doing almost nothing at all, everything was explodingly vital!

Tocco broke my reverie. 'They do very little but look and be looked at. Sometimes the tension gets so high in here, though, that all hell breaks loose and there is more sustained fucking and sucking and carrying on than you can imagine. Personally I have always found this particular style a bit tedious, but I can appreciate the purity of line it involves. With a body the size of mine, exhibitionism would verge on the grotesque.' This was the first time I had heard Tocco make any reference to his personal preferences, and it amused me to hear him, of all people, use a word like *grotesque* disparagingly. He nudged my elbow for us to leave, and as I walked out I glimpsed a man squeezed so far down to the floor that his chin was pushed in, looking between the legs of a couple fucking. And as he watched a thick cock thrashing in and out of the stretched churning cunt lips, his eyes grew wide and his face lit up with what surely must have been glowing revelations.

We went diagonally across to a door marked 'Sadist-Masochist,' and I almost hesitated to enter, fearing blood and gore on the other side. Tocco sensed my mood and hastened to reassure me. 'Nothing crude goes on in these corridors, Michael. The people here, although they are engaged in what seems infantile behaviour at times, are quite serious and intelligent. There's none of that silly chain and leather business here. They are all specialists who, like yourself, know what it is to be broken by pain, and it is from that vantage point that they study its effects.'

We opened the door on to what seemed to be a lecture room. A man was standing speaking to a group of about twenty people who sat facing him. It might have been a schoolroom except for two things: they were all nude, and a woman was tied to a long table in front of the speaker. We walked around to the back and joined the audience.

'So,' the speaker was saying, 'it is clear that pain has at least two primary functions – releasing energies within oneself, and serving as a counterweight to the partner's pleasure. The more A suffers, the more B can enjoy himself or herself, and the fuller is A's experience.' He looked down at the woman in front of him, her legs rising to the rich hills of her thighs, her pubic hair bristling up like grass between her legs, and a thin waist flaring up to huge breasts which now sank to either side of her rib cage like great mounds of jelly. 'Barbara here is quite tense in her rectum and abdomen, although she is not ordinarily aware of that. Let us picture what might happen if she went to bed with, as they say on the outside, some man she has come to like.

'As they fuck, she experiences initial pleasure, but as it starts to mount, it is somehow cut off. She doesn't know why, for she is not in contact with the tensions in her body and mind which keep her holding on. Her mind starts to work, and she begins to wonder what is wrong. Perhaps she blames the man, or condemns herself. If he

138

is a typical lout, he is so busy enjoying the simple friction of rubbing his cock inside her cunt to notice anything, and will fuck her until he comes. But if he is somewhat sensitive he will notice that something is wrong and wonder why she isn't enjoying herself fully. Then, if he is an intellectual, he will stop to ask her about it, which will, if he does not possess the utmost empathy, embarrass her and put the two of them through one of mankind's most tedious scenes, the frigidity rigamarole.

'But if he is an activist, he will thrust harder, grab at her, and poke at her. And like a monkey learning his first building blocks trick, he makes a crude cause and effect chain in his mind. He will notice that the rougher he gets, the more responsive she becomes. He will form barely articulate notions like, every time I put my finger up her anus, she starts to go wild, or every time I slap her arse she digs it, or when I pinch her nipples hard, she flips. On her part, she doesn't like pain, but oddly, the more pain there is the more sexual pleasure she enjoys. So an association is made: pain-pleasure. Neither of them has the slightest notion that what is happening is that shock is being used to relax tension, and neither of them has the slightest notion of what true relaxation is. So she becomes what the psychology texts stupidly refer to as masochist. He, on the other hand, gets a bonus, for he has a willing outlet for his aggression and suppressed violence. She pays for what she has been told are sins, via her conditioning from parents, priests, teachers, *et al*. And ultimately, she lets herself be beaten because she is no good, the proof of which is that she can't come. Next thing you know, she's tied to a post and some man is whipping the daylights out of her.'

He took a sip of water and continued, 'Now, the really interesting thing is that knowing that intellectually doesn't make the slightest bit of difference. One has to realise the truth of it. One has to feel pain, and the usually accompanying states of degradation and helplessness (although those are, strictly speaking, different realms), and observe the process as it takes place. With that in mind . . .'

There was in interruption. 'Sir, before you proceed, may I ask what the dynamics of sadism are?'

The man smiled. 'That's quite simple. A sadist is one who does not have the courage to be a masochist, and must take pleasure vicariously, through identification with the victim.' He paused. 'And speaking of victims, today we will have a confrontation between the insides of Barbara's thighs and a lighted cigarette.'

A ripple went through the room as people hunched forward and resettled in new positions. The speaker pulled a pack of cigarettes from a drawer under the table, lit one, and holding it between his thumb and forefinger, leaned forward. Barbara attempted to pull away, and a thin film of sweat broke out on her brow. She twisted towards me and I could see her mouth fall open. Her tongue flickered between her teeth, and she seemed to be inviting us to do something for her or to her. Her buttocks squashed flat against the table top and she drew her pelvis back, sucking her cunt in deep between her legs. The speaker brought the red tip to within a quarter inch of her thigh, close up to the crotch. Barbara began to moan. The man leaning over her gloated, 'I won't do it until you tell me, tell me you want it, tell me you want me to hurt you.' The cigarette tip was almost touching her skin, and a thin wail escaped her lips. 'Tell me you like it,' he pressed on. 'Beg me to do it.' And to my surprise, as she continued trying to pull away, she began to shout. 'Yes, do it! Do it! Burn me, grind it out on my legs! Shove it up my cunt, burn me, burn me!'

The lecturer brought the cigarette close to her pubic hair. 'Do you want it on the cunt, Barbara, shall I mash the flame right into your tender cunt lips?' I found myself trembling in anticipation. Would he really do it?

And at that point, he delicately lowered the cigarette so that it hung right above the white flesh of her inner thigh, just where it begins to flare up and become her cunt. She yowled, 'No, don't, please don't!' But with his

140

other hand, he reached down and inserted two fingers into her box, and began moving them around with violent thrusts. Her body seemed to split in two, as part of her strained towards the hand now ravaging her cunt, and part of her tried to pull back from the cigarette. For an eternity she hung poised, and then with a bloodcurdling scream thrust finally fully forward, taking his hand right up to the knuckles and allowing the glowing red ember to plunge into her flesh.

The speaker immediately pulled out his hand and took the cigarette away. He reached under the table again, took out a bit of gauze and a bottle of ointment, and wiped the burn down gently. He looked up at the audience and said, 'The theoretical ramifications of today's experiment are quite interesting, and I would like each of you to write a short paper on some aspect of the experience. Please pay attention in your writing to the conflict between the fear of actual pain and the symbolic desire to be immolated. That will be all for today.' Then he paused a moment and said, 'If anyone wishes to use her before I untie her . . . she should be prime right now.' There was a moment's hesitation, then several men got up and went over to the table. They looked down at her for a moment, and then all at once swarmed up over her. One glued his mouth to the nipple of her left breast, took the soft globe in his hand and began kneading it very hard with his fingers. A second man climbed between her legs, and without any preliminaries, plunged his cock into her cunt; he rode her shallow and high so that she began to squirm in excitement under him. The other knelt at her shoulders, and teased her mouth with his cock until she began straining to raise her head to reach him, licking at his cock with her outstretched tongue, and imploring him with her lips to drive the hard, long tool into the gulping frenzy of her throat.

Tocco and I stood up and made our way out. I was filled with a rich, deep excitement that was at least sexual, but had more elements in the mix. Most surprisingly, I had no desire to enter into the scene. When we were

141

outside, we looked at each other. 'That's a very strange group of people,' I said. 'Yes,' he answered. 'I rather like them except they tend to be snobs. They have an elitist attitude and consider themselves on the true forefront of sexual experimentation, claiming that pain is the key to all understanding. It's very Eastern, actually.' We went past several doors and then stopped. 'Now here is something a bit different.' I turned to look, and on the door it said: 'Marriage.'

'This,' said Tocco, 'is one of our more flourishing branches of research. Of course, the nuclear family has been an anachronism for almost as long as it has existed, and yet it still has a compelling appeal to people who, one might think, ought to know better. It seems to offer nothing but limitation of freedom, dampening of consciousness, false notions of responsibilty, and a general deadening of vital life forces. It is boring, maddening, inefficient, and perhaps the basic cause of all that is wrong with our civilisation. And yet people still flock to it in millions every year.

'More and more people are discarding it, and the younger ones are showing signs of rejecting it outright. But it does no good simply to condemn the institution. Honestly, all of us, somewhere inside us, want that particular blend of possessiveness and fear and so-called fidelity which can hypnotise us into believing there is some security in this world. Also, since it is at the core of our culture, we are all infected with its attitudes and emotional colouration. And in freeing ourselves of it . . .'

I interrupted: 'Do you think marriage is no good under any circumstances?'

'Of course not. But as with everything else, we must discard our prejudices and images before we can come to terms with the actuality. Marriage is not only possible but potentially extremely beautiful, but to reach that point, we must go through horrors of self-understanding that discourage all but the most hearty. And the first door that must be passed through is jealousy.' He turned the knob on the door. 'Let's look in,' he said.

142

The room had only three people, a woman and two men. Two were obviously a pair, and the second man sat at a distance and watched. There was a sexual tension in the air as thick as water. We arranged ourselves next to one wall and watched. Tocco leaned over and whispered to me, 'The husband has been tortured with feelings of wanting to share his wife with other men, but unable to tolerate the idea. What's happening here is his attempt to work it out in actuality.' I suddenly realised that a number of times Tocco must have exhibited one of my scenes with the same kind of dispassion, and it was very strange being on the observer's seat.

The husband leaned forward and cupped one of the woman's breasts with his hand. She leaned back, and as she did so her skirt rode several inches up her thighs. It was a small movement, but every person in the room was aware of it. The husband licked dry lips. 'Do you want her?' he said to the other man. The second man kept his eyes glued to the woman's thighs and said, coolly, 'The question is, does she want me?' The husband responded, 'I'm the one who's giving her to you; you have to reply to me.'

The second man looked up. 'I don't believe in human property,' he said. 'We make it because she wants to or we don't make it at all.' The husband tried again. 'Do you want me to give her to you?' he said. The intruder answered, 'I don't care about you. I don't want to fuck her to put you down. I just want her. I want her to wrap those beautiful lips around my cock; I want to feel her bottom in my hands; and I want to stick this tool between those pretty thighs and right into her cunt. And you can watch, or leave. I don't care. I just want cunt. What do you want?'

The husband looked desperate. 'We've spent years building a bond of trust and intimacy, and you want to come along and just plunge your cock into the middle of it to destroy what we have together.'

The second man began to inch forward. 'I don't want

143

to destroy anything. I'm not stealing her away from you. I just want to fuck her; why is that so hard to understand?'

Just then, the woman leaned back even further, and let her legs fall apart. Her breasts strained tautly against her blouse. She and the second man looked into each other's eyes, but both were only seeing her cunt, so that as he looked at her, their eyes were just lenses, while the emotions and the consciousness prepared to fuck.

The husband turned to her. 'Is that what you want, Marianne? Do you want to fuck him?'

She looked at him, and pity mingled with a hard centre. 'Of course I want to fuck him. Don't you think I have the same urges you do? Don't you think I want a new cock sometimes, a new smell, a new way of riding? Don't you think I'm thrilled by the notion of having a stranger enter me?'

'I can understand that,' he said, 'but what if . . . ?'

She cut in. 'What if I enjoy him more than I do you? Is that it? Well, what if I do? Who are you to limit my range? The contract I made with you didn't include limiting my sexual freedom. And I am not going to take having you emotionally blackmail me. Besides, this is your idea. I was content until you started filling my head with these notions. And now you're unhappy because I believed you.'

She touched him tenderly on the cheek and said, 'Poor Robert. Why don't we just do it?' He looked up at her, and she began slowly unbuttoning her blouse. She let her skin be revealed by degrees, and then reached behind her to unsnap the brassiere. Her breasts swung out and bounced gently until they came to rest in an easy sag. She looked over at the second man, who replied by stroking the bulge that was showing down one leg. She looked down at the outline of his cock through the tight pants, and her mouth fell open and her eyes grew smoky.

She now lay all the way back, in an open invitation for them to carry it off. The second man crawled forward, and as he came up level with her waist, slid his hand all the way up her skirt until he had grabbed her full on the cunt through her nylon panties. She moaned and turned her head away, but her husband was there, now excited and diving into the realisation of his fantasy with no reserve. He whipped out his cock and met her lips with it as she moved. She reached for it, and he crawled up until her face was cradled between his thighs, with his knees drawn up, and her sucking with small sobs and whimpers.

Concurrently, the other man pulled up her skirt to reveal the lower treasures. Without ceremony, he pulled her panties down. 'No need to warm up,' he said to no one in particular, 'the bitch is hot.' And he poked and wormed in a great eight-inch cock, with a mammoth head, tapering off towards the base. It was shaped like a baseball bat, and as the immense tip ripped through her, her mouth formed a silent 'O'.

The two men rode her together in that fashion. She seemed almost paralysed, although she was enjoying the most overwhelming sensations. The man pushed her legs back, exposing her cunt fully, and while still in her, reached forward and pulled the lips apart even further. Her husband grabbed her by the back of the head and brought her mouth fuller on to his cock. She lay in total transport and sucked like a lapping dog while she let her cunt be rammed and plundered by the stranger's hungry prick.

'Let's turn her over,' the man said, and pulled out only to grab her hips and throw her over on her belly. Her husband slid himself under her so that she could continue working with her mouth, and the man pushed her knees away from him so that her arse rose in the air and exposed all the tender slit from behind. He sank fully into her, and she let out a low groan which was immediately stoppered by the cock entering her throat. The man behind her pulled out again; this time he brought his mouth down between her cheeks and began licking and biting and sucking at the now dripping and gyrating cunt. She rolled her bottom through the air and forced it back so that her cunt was forced more fully on to his mouth. The motion transferred to her mouth, and she began sucking with

145

passion, until her husband's knees buckled and his pelvis thrust up time after time while a mouthful of sperm was delivered, and she gobbled his cock until it was completely drained.

Then everything stopped for a moment. The husband seemed stunned, and his wife just opened her mouth to let the limp cock fall out. Behind the woman, the second man straightened up, and his cock stood out, still stiff and ready for action. The situation froze in an instant of terrible clarity. The husband had come and was now out of it, and it was easy to see the question flit over his face as to whether she had sucked him off simply to get him out of the way, so she could enjoy the other man without distraction.

She was watching his face, and then, with the slightest shrug of the shoulders, pushed her buttocks back so that her cunt slipped like a perfectly fitting glove over the waiting cock. The man pushed her sideways, and then swung one leg around so she was facing him. She let out a single sob and flung her legs high in the air and wrapped them around his shoulders. He sank into her like a tyre which has suddenly been punctured, and let himself ride on the wide ocean of delirium tossing beneath him, being bounced about on a constantly shifting, changing hot sea of sensation and feeling, looking down from time to time to see the naked face of a woman in the throes of complete abandon. He flung his arms to the side and thrust forward so that he penetrated her heavily and directly from above. She bucked under the stimulation and emitted a series of low grunts that changed into gasps, as though she couldn't catch her breath, and then a long undulating wail that made the hair on my neck prickle, until she was digging into his shoulders with her nails and slamming at his body with her entire body, her cunt working like a hungry mouth, enveloping his cock and sucking at it, demanding, when, with a hoarse cry of release, she shuddered against his body and, still clinging, pumped wave after wave of throbbing cunt into his cock.

He came quietly, softly, with a look of reverence and surprise on his face.

They lay locked for a long time and gradually straightened their limbs and stretched out their bodies, and rolled apart. After a while they sat up and smiled at one another in a kind of secret understanding. Suddenly, the spell was broken by the voice of the husband. 'You never came that way with me,' he said. He was sitting with his arms curled around his knees and looked like a sulking four-year-old child. The lovers gave each other a 'what can we do?' look, when Tocco hoisted himself up on his feet and lumbered over to the unhappy man like a rhinoceros preparing to charge. He went right up to him, and to everyone's surprise, yanked his head up by the hair and slapped him soundly across the face.

'You have one choice, my friend, and the choice is NOW. There is no one, not one single person in the known universe, who will help you when you want to suffer. And it doesn't matter how many rationalisations you have, or how many reasonable arguments for your case; if you can't cope with whatever reality is coming down, you will go under.' Tocco spoke with fire in his eyes. 'So, will you face the stupidity of jealousy and possession, and end it, now, once and for all, or will you slide back into that morass of sentimentality and oppression which is lovingly called the family? There's no compromise. If you succumb to jealousy, there's no way out.'

The husband seemed to gather strength from Tocco's words. 'I want to be rid of it, you know that,' he said, 'but I don't know what to do.'

Tocco looked around at the other two. 'Well,' he said, 'it seems that those two have something fairly exciting happening between them now, and have no immediate need of a third. So why don't you go take a walk?'

The indecision showed itself as a field of conflicting movements over his face. Tocco bent down to him again. 'That is the reality. Do you understand? The reality. She is hot for another man. There is no way you can change that. There is no way you can convince her not to feel that. Your only strength lies in letting it happen and then seeing what comes next. You can't pin her down to a tomorrow. If the two of you have something worthwhile, you will be together enough.'

The husband stood up slowly and looked down at his wife, and a strange sense of power radiated from him. She watched him and her face seemd to grow ten years younger, as though she were a young woman again and seeing him for the first time. The man at her side fell out of the ring of attention. Then Tocco did something of true mischief. He said to the husband, in a loud whisper, 'Besides, there are scores of eager-cunted girls and women crawling – sometimes literally crawling – over the grounds outside.' The husband smiled, turned on his heels, and walked out.

The woman made a gesture as if to follow him or call out to him, but the man behind her reached around and pulled her down. He covered her tits and began mauling them, pinching at the nipples. The door slammed shut, and after a moment's shock she turned to her new lover, and with a look of self-disgust, flung her mouth down to his cock.

Tocco took my elbow and we left the room. 'They've been doing this for weeks now,' he said. 'Jealousy is not like syphilis. It takes more than a shot of penicillin to cure it.'

We got out into the hallway, and Tocco continued. 'I think we've had enough for today. I'm afraid I've become a little tired. It's still amazing to me that people demand comfort from one another, as though it could be given on request. If only people would be simple in knowing precisely what they wanted, then they could ask for things it is reasonable to expect that others can provide: a glass of water, a bit of privacy, a good fuck.' He paused, and added with a flourish, 'But the species has never been known for its ability to do anything simply.'

We ascended in the elevator, and Tocco said, 'You are in a different place than you were when you got here, and

148

I have let you have some time simply to enjoy your new awareness. But you have yet to come to terms with the specifics of your original question. And for that, I will introduce you to VuVu. But get a good night's sleep, and I will come by for you in the morning.'

We went into his study, and I had started to leave when something tripped in my mind, and I asked, 'Tocco, what do you get from all this?' He looked at me with an amused smile for a long while, and then said, 'How else would a fat, ugly old man get so much sex?'

I spent the day walking in the woods. Spring was setting the juices free, and the trees became more alive, and the afternoon filled with the sounds of men and women fucking on the grass.

CHAPTER THIRTEEN

I got up early the next day, just after the break of dawn, and went to the kitchen for a solitary breakfast. I felt strong and clearheaded, and looked forward to meeting the woman Tocco had spoken about, VuVu. I wondered if she were French.

I went back to my room and spent a pleasant hour just sitting in a wicker chair at the edge of the garden, watching the day come alive. I don't know when I had been more content. And when Tocco's knock came at the door, I was positively exuberant in greeting him. But once again he pulled the rug out from under me, for he was dressed in a dark blue double-breasted suit, complete with a bowler hat and thin briefcase. His black leather shoes squeaked as he walked in. His tone was extremely brisk.

'What you will be doing today,' he began, 'is confronting yourself in a way not available to man prior to the past twenty years. And there have been perhaps only a dozen people in the world who have attempted this experiment. They have all failed. Two committed suicide, one went mad, and the others reported that they were totally untouched by what happened. So I have high hopes for us today, for if you can deal with VuVu, it will provide our research with a first. And, in a way I am not allowed to divulge, our funds depend on our continuing success. But there's no point in talking about it further. Let's be off.'

We went once more through his office and down the elevator, but this time, upon emerging, we took the hallway to the right. I wondered what sort of woman she must be to merit all this special attention, and just what sort of esoteric trip she had that was new to mankind's experience. We finally came to a small wooden door, opened it, and entered into a medium-sized room. Tocco turned on the light and a strange sight met my eyes. In the centre of the room was a massage table. Above it hung a strange set of pulleys and metal arms and rubber tubes. One wall was a bank of meters and circuitry housing, while four video screens stared down from the ceiling. It looked in a way like a surreal recording studio.

I turned to Tocco. 'Where's VuVu?' I said. 'You're looking at her,' he answered. My mind went quizzical. Tocco's eyebrows went up and his face showed a flash of sudden understanding. 'Oh, how foolish of me. Of course, you would have had no way of knowing. VuVu is a computer.'

I laughed. 'Tocco, you're not going to sit me down for a battery of psychological tests, are you?'

He spoke slowly. 'I don't know quite how else to put this, Michael, but you are going to have sex with VuVu.'

And then it made sense. The contraption above the bed brought to mind descriptions of the Masters and Johnson machinery. The mechanical aspects were clear, but what was the role of the computer itself?

Tocco seemed to be reading my thoughts. 'VuVu is programmed to understand body language. Instead of dealing with problems of physics or economics or space flight, or some other inane area of human activity, we have fed all the variables of body language into the computer, using a series of equations which make a kind of sexual unified field-theory.'

I was startled. 'Where do you get mathematicians of that calibre, Tocco?' I had a paranoid flash. 'Are you being supported by the CIA?' I demanded. 'It's rather more international than that,' he answered.

'Some of the variables are simply physiological, heart rate, blood pressure, skin temperature, muscle tonus, and so on. Others refer to a language of gesture, facial expressions, angle of limbs, speed of movement, et cetera. VuVu can respond to the spoken word, so anything you say will be part of the material. And also, we shall have tiny electrodes pinned to your scalp to measure changes in brain wave function.

'VuVu will be doing a number of things simultaneously. One is to analyse all the data you provide her in order to produce a sexual profile for you. Also, she will be controlling the mechanical cock and cunt which you seen hanging down from the ceiling. In short, you will be fucking and being fucked by a computer programmed to give you a perfect lay, and at the same time let you know what your scene is.'

I looked at the set-up with a measure of respect. Tocco rubbed his hands together and said, 'Let's begin.' He snapped his fingers and two women dressed as nurses came into the room: Susan and Sylvia. I was told to take off my clothes, and then I lay down on the table. A number of switches were thrown and the room lights dimmed except for a bright glow in the centre where I lay. The television screens went on, and four images of me stared down at me from the ceiling. The computer lit up with several dozen green and red lights, and the nurses busied themselves making sure the machinery above me was working and lubricated. Then Syliva pulled down a number of thin wires and began pinning them on to my scalp. 'They're quite loose,' she said, 'so you don't have to worry about moving your head.'

And then, suddenly, all the preparations were over. I lay naked and ready, waiting for the computer to make its move. Susan came over and squeezed my hand. 'Whatever happens,' she said, 'I'll be waiting for you afterwards.' To my surprise, I found myself saying,

155

'Please Susan, the melodrama makes the scene a bit over-ripe, don't you think?' She began to look hurt, but I smiled at her, and she copped to it. 'I hope you die, you prick' she said, then kissed me and left. The others followed, and standing at the door, Tocco said, 'Whenever you are ready, there is a little switch by your right hand which will start things going. You will also find something to relax you in the drawer under the table by your left side. Good luck.' And with that, he left the room.

I lay there for a moment, and then found the drawer he mentioned. In it were a number of joints and some matches, and a supply of poppers. I rolled to my side, and getting comfortably propped up on one elbow, I lit a joint. Immediately, I began to relax, and after a while lay back again to look things over.

Within a short time I felt an odd sensation creeping up on me. It was a sense of aloneness without really being alone. The images of myself on the screens gave a sense of otherness, although the other was still me. Watching myself in such objective immediate feedback did strange things to my head. And then, the images changed, and it took a moment for me to realise that what was happening was that three of the screens were showing pictures of me in a different time-space. One seemed to be five minutes behind, another was a minute or so, and the third was about fifteen seconds. It must have a delayed feedback loop being used, and it provided a disoriented twist to my time sense.

And then I became aware of the living wall of lights, and I remembered the reality of the computer, a mass of electrodes and wires and transistor circuits. It was only a machine, of course, but then, so was I. In many ways it was much more intelligent than I was, and although I knew it wasn't a person, a sense of quiet and precise awareness emanated from the wall. VuVu sat in perfect self-absorption, not needing or wanting anything, not caring to budge, not evaluating, but simply being aware and analysing whatever data came through. I saw in an instant that it was nothing other than the Buddha mind, and that man had created a machine which exhibited all the faculties of perfection he himself had only occasionally been able to achieve.

Suddenly I was turned on to the whole thing. I could do or say anything I wanted with VuVu, and it would be dealt with impartially, with no distortion. I lit another joint and let myself become open to the machine. If the computer could give me back myself in my relationship with it, if it helped me to know myself better, then it was obviously the organism that I needed to involve myself with. I finished the joint, lay back fully, and threw the switch.

Immediately the machinery above me began to move. The first thing which descended was a penis substitute, a cunningly carved cock made of some material that came close to feeling like skin. It came down to the level of my thighs and nudged itself right under my balls. I lifted my legs; the cock slid down the crack of my buttocks and moved towards my arsehole. Somewhat self-consciously, I guided my body so that the cock went right to the hole, and then it began gently prodding until it entered. The effect was pleasant, but not electrifying. I did a few experimental wiggles, found the cock to be pliable, and opened to it more. I caught sight of myself in the screen, and for a moment I appeared totally ludicrous, but that changed to flashes of depravity, and the image-war began in my mind. But this time I just let it rage, not getting involved in identifying with any of the ideas, but simply letting them be part of the experience.

Then the cock inside me began to swell, and I realised that it was flexible as to size. It grew larger and larger until I thought it could fill me no further. My anus stretched tight around its immense width, and the tip of it penetrated deeper than any man ever had. But there was no pain at all. I heard myself sighing, and I grabbed my ankles to let the cock slide deeper into my now totally spread arse. With that, it began to get hotter. The temperature of the cock increased until I felt my bowels begin to flush with heat. The temperature rose until I almost felt scalded, but at the same time I felt myself yielding and letting myself be penetrated more than I had thought possible. It must have been in me a foot and a half, and was now tingling hot, when it began to move. I snapped a popper, and sank into total passive acceptance, to enjoy what has, even to this date, been the best fuck of my life.

The cock went in and out, moving through its entire vast length. It pushed to the sides; it teased the rim of my anus, and then plunged into the very root of me. It tipped in at dozens of angles, and I reached down to spread my cheeks even more. I opened inside forever. I couldn't open enough. I pushed against the cock and begged for more. For deeper. For hotter. The popper heightened all the sensations, so that I could feel the ripples going up and down the canals past the opening to my arse.

And just when I thought nothing more could happen, the cock began to vibrate in a soft, rapid rhythm. I fell apart, and split right down the centre. If the cock had changed to a knife at that point and penetrated me, I would have welcomed it. And I realised that what allowed me to feel thus was that VuVu wouldn't hurt me: the computer was only interested in seeing how far I went, and how. The cock was probably sensitised and would not penetrate if there was too much tension, and would stop if it were asked. So I could open, and did. I closed my eyes and let myself be fucked for a long rapturous time, sailing into that region past the reach of understanding, deep into the brute fact of unformed living consciousness. I cried and moaned and thrashed my head wildly about, and at the moment when the pressure on the prostate gland reached the point that I spilled into coming, I voluntarily reached up to embrace my partner and opened my eyes in horror when my arms wrapped around a tangle of pipes and struts and wires.

In a flash I saw that I had become so enraptured with the sensation that my concentration had strangled attention, and I had forgotten all the other elements of the moment. At the point of complete abandon, there was nothing to hold on to but machinery. A familiar feeling of nausea welled up in my stomach, but at that moment the sounds of my fucking began to be played back, and I looked up to see myself on the screens, in various stages of passion, opening my legs, yearning towards the cock. I stared in wide-eyed wonder, and grasped the point, that the act did not end when I came, that the act went on forever, reverberating through time and space, always recorded, always having an effect. And the important thing was the sex, the actual fucking, which had been visiting me for a while, and was now visiting millions of people throughout the world. And I flashed the vision of a vast field of bodies, in a giant orgiastic tumble, with all the cunts that have existed since the monkeys first appeared, in all their shapes and sizes and smells. And the billions of cocks, all hard and pulsing with desire. And wave after wave of posture rolling over the field of flesh, in every conceivable shape and form until there was nothing but a great fucking and sucking and eating and caressing and slapping.

Then I felt a problem crack open, and I realised why I was often so sad after the orgasm, why I retreated. It was because I treated the moment of orgasm like a museum piece which, once perfected, should be hung on the wall of memory and revered. And in doing that, I missed the continuation of the flow, the moment-to-moment change. So much intensity goes into orgasm, that like a heavy body, it bends light around it, distorting all vision for some time afterwards. But with seeing this, I could just lie back and let awareness continue, and drift into the flow of my body's ebb, and accompany with my mind the travels of sex as it whipped through the world, enlivening individuals and tripping them into one another's arms.

Tocco's words came home: 'The point is to not swing wildly from extreme to extreme all the time, but to know a quiet awareness at the edge where the opposites are constantly interpenetrating. Then you will be silent inside. Then you will understand.'

As I lay thinking, another arm of the machine descended, and this time at its tip was a disembodied cunt. Again, it was an almost perfect sculptural imitation, covered with natural hair. But it looked very eerie descending as it did at the end of a metal arm. I wondered if Dali had had a hand in the design, when the cunt came down and completely covered my cock. It gave off a smell that was indistinguishable from real cunt; it pulsated with vibration and gave off heat, so that in a moment I felt my cock stiffening to rise into it.

The cunt grabbed my cock like a hand. And began to move up and down, and around, thrusting and drawing back, always returning to the base of my cock to long slow pull up to the head. I lay back to enjoy it, and soon began to move in unison with it. Perversely, I grabbed the metal arm so that I could pull the cunt in closer to me, and began to ram into it hard, sloshing around inside, stretching the walls, bruising the lips. I could be as rough as I wanted, knowing that I wasn't causing pain. And the thought went through my mind whether fucking a computer wasn't the best sex possible, a kind of ramified masturbation.

VuVu responded, and soon we were moving into each other, and peaking in cycles, only to descend to come at it again. I was moving in an oddly familiar way when I realised that I was fucking the cunt the way the cock had just been fucking me! That I had learned, through my responses to being fucked, more about fucking! The notion was so simple, I wondered how I could have overlooked it all this while. The better a woman I became, the better a man I could be, yet to do that, I would actually have to experience the sense of being a woman while I was being fucked, even though I knew all about the womb fantasy now and how I really wasn't a woman. But then, when I went to bed with women, did I suddenly switch roles to become a man? The whole thing danced around in my head, with confusion between social roles and inner images and sexual organs and having children.

To complicate matters, VuVu dropped the cock substitute again, and as I groaned into the cunt now hanging over the head of my cock, teasing it with its heat and juices, the computer's cock sank down and smoothly lodged itself between my cheeks and into my anus. I went wild with the effect. All the ambivalences in me coalesced in a single unifying movement. The cock moved into me and brought me to a state of utter abandon, and with that same abandon, I plunged into the cunt wrapped around me. I no longer had any label to hang on to what was happening. One might have called it a bisexual experience, but that would have missed the richness of it, the exquisite subtleties. My body was like an alchemist, taking the metal of the cock going into my arse and transforming it into the metal of my cock going into the cunt. In a real sense, VuVu was fucking herself, but I was a catalytic agent, translating one input into an output so totally restructured as to be a different thing.

At one point I lost all sense of what was there. My cock felt as though it was the cunt and the cunt was a cock driving into me. My arse became a cunt, and the cock going into me became a cock growing out of my cunt and going into someone else's arse. Then it didn't matter at all, and the only thing left was the heat and the dance of the organs and the growing climax. I let myself go totally passive, and in that found the centre of activity.

We fucked for ages, and I popped a dozen poppers and watched myself freak out over four spots in time, and rode with it until I could contain myself no more and let the scalding spunk rise in spurts up the tube and shoot into the gaping cunt that hung down from the ceiling, and simultaneously felt the cock discharge a hot sticky fluid deep inside my arse.

I fell back, closed my eyes, and relaxed more totally than I ever had in my life. The cunt and cock stayed glued to me for a very long time, and then gradually they pulled away, and I was left by myself on the table in the middle of the room.

However, in a few minutes, the lights on the computer

161

wall began to blink in absurd patterns, and I realised that everything that had happened was being run through and analysed in a process that I could not begin to understand. I got off the table, disengaged the electrodes, stretched luxuriously, and dressed.

Tocco came back in.

'From what I can judge to date, the entire thing was a success. How do you feel?'

I checked myself. 'Perfect,' I said. 'It was dazzling.'

'Did you learn anything?' he asked.

I told him about my realisations, but there was more somehow that I couldn't put into words. It was that part that he was interested in. 'The next step is dangerous, for VuVu will provide you with the words to describe that area of experience which is now blank. The danger is that you will take the words as a solution to the problem, when all they do is to close the gap in your mind, complete the gestalt as it were. When the last piece of the conceptual puzzle is in place, then you can forget all further verbal considerations about sexuality, and begin to live yourself fully.'

I felt piqued. 'Isn't that what I've been doing?'

'Yes, you have. And in addition, you have been muddying your perception with the search for understanding. What you haven't realised is that the search itself was the source of confusion. Once you know there is nothing more to know, then you can begin to learn.'

'That last sentence just spun my head around,' I said.

'Well, let it settle then. We can go to my study, and when VuVu's analysis is translated into English, we'll take a look at it.'

CHAPTER FOURTEEN

We settled in the study, and Tocco brought out some glasses and a bottle of brandy. He took off his jacket, loosened his tie, and heaved himself onto the couch by the window. I drew up an easy chair and sat facing him. He poured the brandy, and we clinked glasses. I felt the velvet liquid burn down my throat and heard Tocco's gasp of pleasure.

I peered at him over the rim of my glass and said, 'Who are you, Tocco?'

He chuckled in the best Sidney Greenstreet manner and put his glass down. 'If you're thinking in terms of my biography, Michael, I shall have to disappoint you. Where and when I came from and developed is a closed book. Basically, I am just a man, who happened to have been born with a good brain and a completely unwieldy body. It didn't take long for me to find out that the pain of unrequited sexual desire surpassed all others in my hall of unhappy experiences. And since I'm a fanatic at heart, I dived headfirst into the area which gave me the most trouble, determined to master it. I mastered the area, all right, but have never come to terms with the pain which comes from desire which isn't reciprocated. I realise that it is a trivial aspect of the self, but we each bear our particular cross with as much dignity and humour as we can manage.'

He shifted his weight and continued. 'But this is not to talk about me. The point is to go into your question, and to see if we can discover what lies at the root of your supposed problem. You came, originally, because you wanted to know if it were possible to share an image orgasm with someone. How do you feel about that now?'

It seemed such a long time ago, and in a way the question made no sense to me now. 'It seems that it was a false problem. After the thing with VuVu I feel that I have to accept my own fantasies for myself, and let the other person have his or hers, and be content with what happens between our bodies.'

'That's a totally pat answer, and doesn't strike to the heart of the situation. Let's take it from the beginning. Fantasy is what happens when there is a conflict in reality that is conditioned and unconscious. When two people fuck, their motives, their emotions, their bodies, all clash. It is a violent bringing together of two autonomous biospheres. Each of the individuals must be in total contact with his or her own reality in order to know what the other's reality is, and only then is there a chance that they can get into complementary rhythms. And the rhythms must be in tune if they are to go into the next stage of self-forgetfulness.

'This is the reason, parenthetically, why an orgy which isn't a jolly group-grope on one hand, or a programmed scenario on the other, requires a number of individuals with enough sensitivity, humour and strength to allow themselves to enter into the chaotic sequences which make the psychic space turbulent before they get it together.

'Now whenever there is unconscious conflict, or unresolved conscious conflict, thoughts are produced, and in the context of fucking, the thoughts take the shape of fantasies of one form or another. Sometimes one enters a mythical realm and transmogrifies into fabled beasts; sometimes the mind grows demonic, and hateful paranoid delusions cloud everything over. The fantasies grow like dank flowers in the stagnant back-water of energy which

166

gets trapped and can't flow. Quite often these flowers are more interesting than the mundane reality which we find ourselves. And one can spend his entire life sniffing imaginary flowers. Many have done so, and in times like these, when an entire civilisation is in full decay, it becomes modish. That, of course, is decadence.

'But for most of us, fantasy is something that comes and goes, and sometimes it's a pleasant movie and sometimes it's a nightmare. And we often fall into the fantasy, identify with its workings, and in its grip attempt to negotiate through reality. Of course, we always stub our toe or plunge off cliffs.'

'How can it be eliminated, then?' I asked.

Tocco frowned. 'You know better than that, Michael. The point is not to try to do anything about the things which our minds produce, but just to watch them, with all the unconcern that we would have in watching a sunset or a tree. In that state, all fantasies become decorations for the fact, and then you may pick one of the flowers and put it in your hair, that is, make a social game of it. Or study it. Or ignore it. Doing this breaks down the effort to deal with fantasy and allows more energy to flow, and you experience a greater reality content.'

I must have looked puzzled, for Tocco quickly interjected, 'Don't take the terms "reality" and "fantasy" to mean two different things, for, of course, everything is real, or unreal, or both, or neither. We must confine our attention to the psychological level, where we form our attitudes or our approach to phenomena, and not waste time trying to decide philosophically what it is we are approaching. Speculations on the nature of reality are really too infantile to discuss.

'Relating this to you, we remember that you were concerned that your partner have the "same fantasy" that you were having. But this is to make a series of false distinctions. First, that there is such a thing as *you* and *another*. In a sense, there is only one of us at all and when we fuck, we fuck ourselves, or, increasingly, fuck ourselves up. The second distinction is between what's going

167

on in your head and what's going on in your body. You have a compulsive file clerk in your mind which takes all phenomena and begins to classify them under such labels as "thought", "emotion", "sensation", and so forth. But there is only one process. Actually, when you are fucking someone, both of you are having the same fantasy, and the same reality, and it is called existence. Any subdivision is pedantic.'

I looked at him admiringly. 'Tocco, you are a smart sonofabitch.'

He shifted his gaze and looked at me shrewdly. 'I think the lecture I just gave you is worth at least a blowjob,' he said.

I blinked. Another trick? A joke? I looked at him again. His face was serious and open. But his eyes were filled with taunting and mockery. I began to grow angry. I was feeling very comfortable, very intellectual, much like a student in private conference with a good teacher, and this intrusion seemed vulgar and gratuitous. Tocco smiled. 'What's the matter, Michael. Getting too enlightened for some cock?'

I rose out of the chair almost without knowing it. I knelt down in front of him and opened the zipper to his pants. I reached in through the opening in the jockey shorts and took his cock out, now flaccid and small. There was no desire in me at all, and I held the tool in my hand as though it were slightly repulsive. And then I got very embarrassed. 'Look, at me, Michael,' Tocco said. I looked up. 'See if you can just suck a cock and not make a big deal out of it. See if you can, for once in your confused life, find out what it is, instead of what you think it should be, or connecting it to some silly image of yourself, or thinking that you have to enjoy it or dislike it. Just do it.'

And then it felt as though a heavy hand were pushing the back of my head down, forcing my face to his crotch and my open mouth to take in his cock. I held it gingerly on my tongue for a moment and felt it begin to stir. Immediately, all the connections began to fall into place,

168

and I went through all the memories that began with the first touchings I did with children in my neighbourhood, to the wildest of scenes in which I was saturated with cock. And as the immense Gothic edifice rose in my head, the simple, plain organ hardened in my mouth, and I found myself gently sucking at it and licking the rim in an easy, loving rhythm.

I realised that this was giving Tocco pleasure, but it was not myself doing something to him. Rather, it was *us* in an act which each of us entered into for our own reasons, and took from it our own treasures. I wrapped my fingers around the base of it and gently tugged it towards me while moving my mouth in opposition to my hand, so that I was pulling it off into my mouth, and using my mouth to create a sensation enveloping it from the other direction.

I lapsed into a dreamy reverie, then heard the voice of Tocco cut through the mists. 'The cock, Michael, don't forget the cock.' Something about the tone of his voice stirred a memory in me. I saw a lost frightened child in a huge train station. He was searching for his parents, but kept getting knocked about in the crowd of rushing thousands. He wanted to scream, but no sound came, and the impulse caught in his throat. Simultaneously, I felt Tocco's cock begin to budge the back of my mouth and enter into my throat.

The memory dissolved into fantasy, and I was in a forest. Up on a ledge a great antlered deer appeared, noble and wise. It was the king of the forest. My knees trembled, and at my ear a large doe nuzzled me. She said, 'Don't be afraid. It's safe now.' Again Tocco's voice cut through the haze, saying, 'Take it all the way in, Michael. You won't choke. Just let your throat get as soft as a cunt.'

I pushed forward and took the cock deep into my throat. It seemed to fill my entire being, and I tingled with energy. I moved in large cycles, going all the way down on the cock and holding it there, letting my throat convulse around the tip, and then pulling back as the cock was sucked back the entire length of my mouth, with my

169

tongue tracing a line down the long, soft underpart. I could feel that Tocco was near to coming. He began to move his pelvis and was talking, half to me, half to himself: 'Come on, Michael, do it, suck it, get it up.'

And with that, the scene changed in my mind. There was a fire in the forest, and I was hurt. The flames crept closer, but I couldn't move. Suddenly the great deer bounded by my side. 'Get up,' he said. 'Get up, Bambi, you must get up.'

And at that moment, Tocco cut loose and sent a long series of pulsing jets into my mouth, and as I swallowed, I suddenly saw the ludicrousness of the entire scene, me sucking off a crazy old fat man while Freudian projections of Walt Disney danced in my head; the incongruity welled in me like a geyser until I could contain it no more, and I fell back and laughed and laughed and laughed until my sides hurt. Tocco began guffawing, and then he too broke out into deep booming laughter. We were like that for a long time, rolling back and forth and exploding in mirth which would subside until we looked at one another again, and pointed at each other and seeing the absurdity, began to roar once more. And after a while I subsided and lay still. Tocco looked down at me, with eyes of pure beaming love and said, 'Michael, you are the funniest cocksucker I have ever met.'

There was a discreet knock at the door. We were both startled, and I got off the floor while Tocco zippered up his pants. 'Come in!' he shouted.

In came a thin, efficient-looking man with a small portfolio. He laid it on Tocco's desk and said, 'The report from the computer,' and left.

Tocco moved behind the desk and sat down, while I pulled up a chair next to him. It was much the same position as when I first arrived. He opened the folder and began reading silently for a minute, and then looked up at me. 'The largest part of this is introduction, which is mostly a series of pre-programmed phrases and ideas that get reassembled for each person depending on the situation. So I apologise in advance for the hackneyed sound of some of this. I'll only read excerpts, and leave out all the physiological data. You can see that if you like.' He looked down again and began reading.

'There is no permanency; all is motion. And we must step conscious into existence. At the heart, there is mystery, and that is part of what we must understand.

'One fucks, one wishes to be fucked; one sucks, one wishes to be sucked; one beats, one wishes to be beaten.

'We are always two. The relationship between the two forms the third. After three, things get complicated.

'Thoughts are endless and limited. It is an activity without profit. Understand the structure of thought. Eat when you are hungry and be aware of your teeth when you chew.

'Labels are to be used, but be careful they do not cover up the contents of the jar.

'Suck a cock on Monday, fuck a cunt on Tuesday, lick an arse on Wednesday, fondle a child on Thursday, dress in women's clothes on Friday, get pissed on Saturday night. Sunday is God's day; make no plans.

'These are interestng times. There is no way to discriminate between decadence and freedom. Violence prevails.

'Love does not speak. Love is.'

Tocco put down the paper and looked at me.

'Sounds like a long-winded fortune cookie,' I said.

'There's one more section,' he added. He made full dramatic use of the moment, and then said, 'Subject is a male lesbian.'

I went halfway between a titter and a snort of protest. And then I settled back in my chair. 'For some baroque reason, Tocco,' I said, 'that makes stunning sense. But don't ask me to explain what it means.'

'A definition is given by the computer. It says: "A male lesbian is a genital male who allows that part of his psycho-social structure which is female to come alive in action, emotion, and thought." Does that clarify the concept?'

I thought about it for a while, then began musing out loud, 'A man, who, if he were a woman, would be a lesbian. Thus, the female in me desires other women. But when I am with them, I am physically a man. When the man in me is living, then I work perfectly with a woman. But if a woman goes to bed with me expecting male cues, and I throw her female cues, we don't get it together. Unless she is also a lesbian, or at least bisexual. So, I try men when I am feeling womanly. But I am now a lesbian making it with a man, which is a drag, unless the man happens to be a homosexual, that is, someone who likes to fuck with men. Then I let him use my body while the woman in me draws forth the woman in him.'

I leapt up. 'Of course, that explains everything! It's obvious!' And no sooner had I said that than I remembered that those were the words Tocco had spoken to me in the wood that day when all seemed so clear. Now it wasn't that things were any clearer, but that the clarity permeated to a greater depth.

'Freud said,' remarked Tocco, 'that the sexual act includes four persons. He might have added, "at least up to the point at which I stopped counting." What you have here is just a key to open the first major door to your understanding of yourself, including your sexual self. It is as though you were a painter and now, after five years, you have finally mastered the rudiments of making a line. Without this tool you can do nothing; but it is only a tool for the real work which lies ahead.'

He seemed so solemn that I had to twit him. 'Do I get a diploma, Doctor Tocco?'

He smiled to himself a moment, and then looked at me. His eyes were alive with inner movements that were reflected in the almost imperceptible ripplings of wrinkles under his eyes. 'I think you are ready to meet someone whom you may not understand until many years from now. That is, you will think you know her and she will seem to teach you much, but for a long time the depth of her impression on you will work in your mind and heart.

Why don't you go take a rest and get something to eat, and later I will show you how to get to Bingo Katy's.'

The name arrested me, and I wanted to know more, but Tocco shoved the computer read-out to me and waved me out of the room. I walked out into the garden and spent an hour reading and thinking over what the electronic brain had read into my behaviour and experience.

CHAPTER FIFTEEN

The day passed quickly as I sat and read. My mind was like a pinball machine, with lights flashing over the board and bells ringing, and every once in a while the whole thing going TILT, and blowing up whatever fancy structure had been building itself in my thoughts. Among other things, I saw the role of the third person clearly for the first time. A person alone mates with a second for completion. But the two then need a third to give them definition. Thus the eternal triangle, whether that meant a mutual friend, or a lover, or a child. It suddenly seemed apparent that the ideal marriage would have to have at least four people, so that subgroups of three could be formed, as well as allowing three different sets of two.

I read and thought all through dinner, which I barely tasted, and the next thing I knew, Tocco was standing by me. 'If you are finished eating, Michael,' he said, 'we can take a walk to Bingo's. It will take us about fifteen minutes.'

We went out and into the woods, and followed a small path for a quarter of an hour until I could see a light. It was a tiny house completely off by itself, and it was built in Japanese style. A dim light shone through the rice-paper in the doors and windows, and a cheap radio was playing big-band dance music. 'This is as far as I will take you. Just go on in through that large door, and there will probably be some people to show you around.' He patted me on the shoulder and then left abruptly.

I stood and watched the scene for a few minutes, and then slowly made my way to the entrance. As I approached I could hear loud voices that sounded as though their owners were drunk. It seemed strange, but I continued until I went through the door and found a small courtyard leading to three wooden steps. At the bottom of the stairs were a dozen or so pairs of men's shoes. I walked over, dropped my shoes, went up the stairs, and entered.

Inside was a small white-washed room with tatami matting on the floor. Nine men sat along the walls, smoking and drinking beer. One of them had on a navy uniform, and one was from the army. They looked up at me and waved me a boozy welcome. I returned a feeble smile and sat down with them. Immediately a young Japanese girl appeared, no older than twelve, and asked me in lisping English whether I wanted a beer. It seemed unpolitic to decline, so I ordered the house special and lit a cigarette. The man sitting next to me leaned over. 'You in the service?' he asked. I shook my head. 'Me neither,' he said. There was a long alcoholic silence. 'You ever get blowed by Bingo before?' he asked. Again, I shook my head. 'Me neither,' he said.

One of the men across the room looked up and shouted, 'Bingo gives the best fucking blow job in the world.' Another man in the corner challenged him. 'She's not as good as Mary,' he said. 'That ugly bitch!' said the first. 'Bingo's prettier,' admitted the second, 'but Mary really likes it. With Bingo it's only a business.'

'Who's Bingo Katy?' I said.

They all spoke at once. 'Who's Bingo Katy? Man, everybody knows Bingo Katy. Where you been? How'd you get here?'

Just then the little girl appeared again, and one of the men went in. A moment later, a different man came out. He stood at the door, held his cock through his pants, and made smacking noises with his lips. Everyone chuckled.

178

He went out and we settled back to wait again. The wait went on for a long time, and a nervous tension filled the room. The navy man began to grumble. 'Why the fuck do we have to wait? She's just a whore. I want to go in when I want to go in.' And he started to crawl towards the door when two of the men jumped on him. The sailor put up a fight, and a scuffle began. Soon there were four men on him, and he was pinned to the floor. One sat on his chest and said, 'You wait your time like the rest at us. If you don't like the way she does it, go someplace else.' The sailor was let up, and he left angrily, cursing and kicking things.

The noise died down and the entrance to Bingo's room opened. I could see the man who had just gone before lying on her bed with his pants pulled down to his knees. And standing in the doorway was the most heartbreakingly beautiful Japanese woman I had ever seen. Her beauty was not in the classic manner, with small lips and thin eyes. Rather she had an open face, and a lush mouth which seemed to be constantly breathing and secreting. She was short, yet had full breasts and widely breaking hips. She clutched a kimono to her chest. 'Is there some trouble?' she asked, and as she spoke, I fell in love with her. With every understanding of all the implications of the situation, my heart nonetheless opened and accepted everything that was, with her as the lens which focused all creation.

She looked at me and her eyes glistened. 'You no come here before, yes?' I felt my heart flutter. 'Yes,' I said.

She swept the room in a glance. 'You all come now,' she said. The men looked at one another for a moment, and then we all lumbered to our feet and stooped into the room next door. 'Today is my birthday,' she said. 'We have a party.'

In a few minutes it was like any party. The beer came out, and I produced grass, which most of the others had never even heard of. And in bits and pieces, I heard the story of Bingo Katy.

She was twenty-four, and at the age of sixteen she got

a brilliant insight into a means of solving her financial future. While her playmates were being girded for some inane job bowing people into department stores, or being readied for marriage to men who would treat them like articulate cattle, she decided to go play with the Americans. She left home and headed for the nearest airbase, where she installed herself in one of the local bars. A pimp picked her up very quickly, and sold her virginity for thirty-five dollars to a hairy sergeant who was willing to pay higher for the privilege of deflowering a teenager. She worked at prostitution for six months until one night a soldier asked her to suck him off. She had not even considered it, and although she had no reason not to, said no. He pleaded with her, and the more he pleaded, the stronger became her resistance. Finally he said, 'I'll give you five dollars more. I won't tell anybody.'

The idea of making money without her pimp's knowing was enough to convince her, and she agreed. He lay back on the bed, and she slid down until her mouth lay opposite his cock. She wondered how she was supposed to do it, and realised she had no idea of what the technique was. So, quite simply, she asked: 'How do you want me to suck?' The question seemed to inflame him, for he squeezed his thighs together. 'Just take it in that juicy mouth, baby,' he said. It seemed simple enough, but she wondered why he was speaking in a hoarse whisper. She leaned forward and let the cock slip between her lips. Not knowing how far it was supposed to go, she let it slide until the tip tickled the back of her tongue. It felt very pleasant, so she kept it there, moving her mouth back and forth very slightly to increase the sensation. The man began moaning and rolling his head from side to side.

She pulled her mouth off the prick and asked, 'You like this?' Again the tightened voice answered, 'Start licking it.' She brought her face down to the deep spot between his legs, and thrust out her tongue into the crack between his cheeks, She licked up very slowly, over his balls, and up the entire length of the cock. When she reached the rim the change in texture stopped her, and she began

180

licking very lightly all around the edge. He put his hands on the back of her head and pushed down. Her head went forward again and her open mouth took the now wet cock all the way to her throat. He pulled her head back, and pushed it forward again. She realised that she had to do nothing but let her mouth stay loose, and he would do all the work, shoving her head back and forth so that the cock plunged and withdrew from her dripping mouth and lips. Finally he began to make deep moaning sounds, and then a mouthful of thick tangy juice spilled on to her tongue. For a moment she was too surprised to do anything, and then, in a gulp, swallowed it. She kept her mouth around his cock for a moment, feeling it go soft, and then pulled away. She looked up at him and said, 'It tastes like orange juice.'

He pulled her up to him and began kissing her, which she now found repugnant. 'Baby, you can suck me off any time,' he said. She regarded him thoughtfully. 'You pay?' she asked. 'Five dollars every time,' he answered. And so her career was born. It was more pleasant, less involving, and more lucrative to suck cocks than to fuck. Also the field was open. There were, as far as she knew, no other whores who specialised in giving head.

She quit her pimp, moved to another town near a military base, and got the nickname Bingo Katy one drunken night of details which she could never remember. For almost eight years now she had been sucking cock day and night, with short breaks for vacation. Her waiting room was always crowded, and she became something of a legend to the Americans who found themselves in Japan.

She told her story, and some of the men told theirs, and we drank and got more warm and friendly, and clothes began to drop off piece by piece. It occurred to me once to wonder where Tocco had found her and how she could continue this incredible performance on his estate. But I was enjoying myself too much to get into questions like that. Whoever she was, she was someone I

181

wanted to know better outside this particular charade, this quaint bit of metatheatre that Tocco had arranged.

'Hey Bingo,' one of the men asked, 'how many cocks have you sucked?' Katy tittered and covered her mouth with her hand. Despite all her hardness, there was still much of the shy young girl about her. One of the other men took up the theme with a certain drunken ponderousness. 'How many men a night?' he asked. She tittered again and then said, 'Maybe twenty, maybe thirty.' She paused. 'When navy ships come in, maybe sixty sometimes.' The thought of blowing sixty men in one night staggered me. 'Let's figure it out,' the ponderous one said. So we took pencil and paper and began multiplying. An average of, say, forty men a night, for about three hundred days a year, for eight years, at six inches per cock, became some ninety-six thousand men, or over nine miles of cock! She didn't understand the figures and we got a dictionary to translate it into Japanese measure. Nine miles! When she understood what that was, her eyes grew wide and her mouth broke into a broad, pleased childlike smile.

We lifted our glasses in a toast. 'Nine miles of cock! Here's to the greatest cocksucker in the world!' And we titled her, 'Blow Queen Bingo Katy.'

We drank and fell into an uneasy silence. The erotic underbelly of the humourous figure began to impinge on our mood, and suddenly we were seven men sitting around half undressed with Bingo on her bed. She sensed that change in mood and became nervous. 'You no gang bang Bingo Katy,' she said, and began to pull back. But there was nowhere to go. 'Let's get her,' said one of the men. And they all reached forward at once to grab her. I sat back and watched. I didn't want to be part of it, and the scene wasn't mine to tamper with.

She started to scream, and one of them put his hand over her mouth. 'We have to tie her down,' he said. Four of them ripped off her clothes and then pinned down her limbs, while the fifth tied a handkerchief over her mouth, and the sixth went to find some rope. He came back, and within minutes she was securely trussed to the corners of her double bed, completely spread-eagled.

Then, as though they felt the impact of what they were doing, they stepped back. For a moment they seemed embarrassed, but Bingo began struggling, and the movement of her body tipped the balance away from rational consideration. Her breasts rolled from side to side, and the cloth cut cruelly into the corners of her mouth. Her gaping cunt twisted as her thighs rocked to and for. Her eyes were filled with terror.

The men slowly began to take the rest of their clothes off. Then one of them reached down and grabbed her hard by the cunt. He took the hair in his fist and yanked it painfully. She bucked back and attempted to moan under her gag. He knelt at her side and began slapping her cunt with his other hand, hitting the tender lips with snapping fingers. One of the other men bent over her and spat copiously into her face, then started slapping her. A third bit at her nipple, holding the tip of it between his teeth and squeezing until I thought he would pop it off into his mouth. The others raked at her flesh with their nails and bit at her thighs.

'Let's give her some beer,' said the one slapping her face, and he took a large beer bottle and shoved it brutally into her cunt lips. The beer spilled into her cunt and began to run out on to the sheet. He dove between her legs and began lapping at the beer as it spilled, and then drew back to shove the bottle all the way into her, past the neck and up to the shoulder, until her cunt would stretch no more to accept it.

She was close to fainting; the man pulled the bottle out and shoved his cock in. The unlubricated cunt protested the dry intrusion, but he forced his way in, burning her lips and cracking with his entire weight into the softness between her legs. Then, to my surprise, he said, 'She's getting hot,' and I could see the first secretions beginning to form on his cock as he plunged it in and out of her now moist cunt. 'Cut her loose,' he said, and the others undid the knots. Immediately her hands flew to his face, fingers aimed at his eyes. He blocked her thrust, and punched her back. 'Sit on her,' he ordered, and one of the other men came up and sat on her face. She turned to one side, and I could see the heavy cheeks of his arse forcing her mouth open while her eyes winked in pain.

But at the same time her legs began to open, and she made small shuddering movements with her pelvis. The cheeks of her arse flattened and dropped full as she shoved the weight of her loins into his cock. Two of the men each grabbed one of her legs, and pulled them wide apart. I thought for a moment they would snap, and the tendons along her inner thigh rose up and formed bridge cables to the opening of her cunt. She was totally spread apart and utterly exposed, and hands and mouths swarmed over her, prodding, kissing.

The first man flung his body into the crevice between her tortured legs, and with a buck and curse, he shot his load into her. And remaining for barely a second, he pulled out, and began punching at her cunt in anger and disgust. 'Hold it,' one of the others said, 'leave some for us.' The man sitting on her got up, and grabbing her shoulders, rolled her over. He put her mouth on his cock and said, 'Start sucking, and if I feel your teeth once I'll knock them all out of your mouth.' She looked at him with horror, and then slowly lowered her head, her tongue pointed out of her mouth, and her lips drawn back over her teeth in an exaggerated curl. Her tongue met the tip of his cock, and then slid down it to the shaft, and the whole thing slowly entered her tentative and probing mouth. She moved up and down a few times, then one of the other men picked up a belt from one of the discarded trousers, and brought it down hard across her buttocks. She flinched but dared not move too much for fear of brushing her teeth against the cock in her mouth. The belt slammed down again, raising reddish welts against the delicate yellow skin. Time and again the belt whacked against the now bleeding cheeks but not for an instant did she lose the delicate balance at her lips. She dug her nails into the first man's thighs, and as tears rolled down her

184

cheeks, she moved her head like a piston up and down on the engorged cock until the man grabbed her hair and shoved her completely down, burying the cock in the pit of her throat, forcing his sperm to spill down her throat. She started to pull away after he came, but he held her there for a full minute, and then I could see a different kind of motion take place as urine spilled up through the same opening and into the back of her mouth, where she drank like a child with its mouth at a water tap. She swallowed all he had inside him, and then fell back.

One by one the others mounted her, one taking her in the anus, causing her to cry out in pain whenever his body slapped against her raw buttocks. Yet another fucked her from behind, and again I marvelled at the mechanism of woman's sexuality, for despite all the terror and degradations involved, the sensation of having a cock in her cunt was enough to start her moving her backside, rotating her thighs in a slow, gentle rhythm. It was as though part of her was mindless, and no matter what the rest of her said, if one put his cock or finger in the right spot, the sexual machine would begin to work.

The gang-bang became desultory. As one man would come, he would go and slump in a corner to drink some beer, and by the time all the others had had a go at her, he would be ready for another round. But by the time of the second orgasm, and after all that beer, erections grew scarce and only three-fourths full. This raised a slow dumb anger in the men, who even at this point were doing manhood trips in terms of how many times they could get their cocks hard, and they forced Bingo into wilder and uglier things in order to get themselves aroused. Someone produced a broomstick and they made her shove it up her anus as far as it would reach. One of them pushed her off the bed and threw her to the floor, where he forced his foot into her mouth, making her lick his toes and painfully squashing her head against the ground.

She seemed in a totally catatonic state, reacting to whatever stimulus was applied, but doing nothing on her own impulse. Her face showed different emotions, but it seemed more like a mask she wore to portray different aspects of a role and had no real connection with what she was feeling, which seemed to be nothing at all. As she was picked up and fucked in the arse, or had a cock shoved into her full mouth and was forced to drink piss or suck the sperm out, as she was taken in the cunt or kicked to the floor, her body twisted in strange and oddly beautiful ways. I was in an almost total haze, because I thought this was yet another reproduction of a scene such as many I had been through, and I remembered how rich and full it seemed from the inside. And from the outside, I could see only brutality and stupidity. Yet, in the midst of it all, Bingo retained a calm and glow that continued to make her incredibly appealing, despite how she came to look.

And in a flash, I saw what it was she was doing. She was acting as the sponge, as the target, for all the vileness and bestiality in these men. She was forcing them to come to terms with the impulses inside them. I thought of her as a human sacrifice in the spirit of sexual knowledge, and on the verge of romantically being carried away by the image, I suddenly became unemotionally disgusted with the whole thing. This was the true perversion in its final form, people putting themselves in situations where their bodies and minds and hearts become mere tools for some supposed inner intelligence which is directing them along some path to enlightenment or salvation or truth. It all seemed so much bullshit. And the proof of it was in the simple observation that there was no joy in this meeting; there was the super-serious concentration of those who have lost sight of the totality of existence. I began to get up to go when one of the men came over to me. 'What's the matter. Don't you want a blow job?' I shook my head. 'Maybe you're too good,' he said in a belligerent tone. He shouted over to the others. 'Hey, this guy thinks he's too good to get a blow job from Bingo.' He grabbed my arm and I pushed him away. I turned to leave when a terrific clout across the back of one ear brought me to my knees. My head spun for a few seconds, and when I opened my eyes, I was surrounded by fists and thighs. I tried to rise very quietly, then all hell broke loose. A hail of fists and feet began crashing about my head and shoulders. I covered up and rolled into a ball, but the punishment continued. I was kicked in the ribs and in the face; someone placed one careful punch into my solar plexus which had me gasping for air, and then I felt a boot grinding my cheek down, forcing my mouth into the floor. All the left-over violence which hadn't gone into Katy now spilled on to me, and for what seemed an eternity I lay there, absorbing the blows and kicks until everything grew black, and I passed out.

I came to with the sensation of cold compresses on my forehead. Bingo was leaning over me with a worried look on her face. I was sore all over, and still fainting. 'You come to bed,' she said, and helped me crawl over and on to the bed, where, as she removed my clothing, I once again sank into unconsciousness.

And when I woke up again it was morning. I was totally stiff over my entire body and each movement caused me to suck in my breath with pain. I turned my head and saw Bingo lying there, looking at me with soft, serious eyes. Through all my discomfort, I felt another rush of tenderness for her as I had last night, and I reached up slowly to touch her cheek. She did not move away, but there was still that odd unresponsiveness which made it impossible to tell what she was thinking or feeling.

'You leave now?' she said. I was taken aback. 'I suppose I can move, but it would be nice just to stay here for a day or two,' I responded. She shook her head. 'I have to clean house, go to store, and pretty soon men begin to come.'

I looked at her incredulously. 'You do this every day?' I asked. She nodded her head up and down. 'Last night was bad time. Most times I just suck. No trouble.'

She looked at me with an appraising glance. 'You want blow job?' she asked.

All of a sudden the charade was too much. 'Come off it,' I said. 'Sure I want a blow job and you can go down

187

on my cock any time you want. But why don't we cut out the bullshit about what you have to do here? I don't know what kind of deal you have with Tocco, but after last night I realise I have to bow to your superior ability to stay cool in the face of shitty scenes. So why don't you drop the phony accent and tell me what you're doing here?'

She looked at me with a totally blank expression, as though she hadn't understood a word I said. 'I no got time for crazy talk,' she said. 'You want me suck you?' I looked at the bruised young body, the full breasts now sagging to one side as she lay propped on her elbow, her hips flaring out into the curves of her hairless thighs, and her tiny cunt bulging out from the joint in her legs. Her mouth had a life of its own, suggesting pleasures no other mouth could offer. I got past caring then, about whether she was putting me on or not, and I pushed her back on to the bed. She looked up at me. 'No rough stuff,' she said. 'Just shut up and open your mouth,' I told her. She closed her eyes and dropped her lips apart. I peered into the open cavern and saw her pink tongue sliding from side to side in anticipation, only to dart out to lick over her trembling lips. Her mouth was stretched as wide as it could go.

I came forward and knelt by her shoulders, and then, sitting on her chest, slowly began to pull on my cock, getting it hard. I felt it expand in my hands and the first rush of warmth raced up and down my thighs. Her breasts made cushions for buttocks and I ground my hips around to roll my backside on her chest. She brought her hands up and ran her fingers over her lips, cupping them at the sides of her mouth. I stayed where I was and continued getting my cock harder. After a while, she opened her eyes and saw what I was doing. She stared at the cock for a moment, so near and yet so removed, and lifted her head towards it. I kept it a few inches away from her waiting lips, now pulling harder, keeping the movement on the shaft from thrashing the head around too much. Her mouth was the target and I didn't want to miss. She trained forward even more and I felt the very tip of her tongue flick at the opening where the load she waited for would come from. The sudden touch of flesh sent warm flashes to my balls, and I grabbed the back of her head to keep her face tilted up, and then leaned my cock forward into the warm, wet, waiting hole. She did almost nothing but allow her mouth to stay soft and inviting, and before I knew it, I was feeling the familiar rising heat in my bowels that signalled the beginning of an orgasm. I wanted to play with her mouth longer, but I had lost, somewhere during the past few weeks, all impulse to prolong or tamper with natural rhythms. If it was time to come, it was time to come. So I let go and let it happen, and my cock filled with melting sensations as she cupped her hands under my buttocks and brought me up and forward to lay my entire cock deep in her mouth as I spent an unusually copious flow into her throat. She clamped her lips around my prick and sucked it all the way from the base to the tip, pulling all the sperm out of the tubes, and then turned her face. I saw what she was about to do and I clamped my hand over her mouth. 'You'd better swallow it,' I said, 'or there's going to be more of what you got last night.' She made a wry face, and then gulped the sticky fluid down.

I got up quickly and set about to dress, which was not easy considering that each movement sent spasms of ache through me. But I got on my shirt and finished buttoning it, while she lay on the bed regarding me coolly. I felt tired and disgusted, with myself, with her, with everything. I turned to leave when she called out to me, 'You pay now.' I spun around and spat out, 'Enough of this shit. You can carry Tocco's charade as far as you like, but I have finished playing. I'll be damned if I'm going to pay you anything.'

I tromped out and sat on the wooden stairs, putting on my shoes, as she shouted after me, 'Goddamn cheap GI! Bingo no suck you again! You no come back here again!' Internally, I gave her an A for sustained performance, and then went out of the courtyard, kicking gravel as walked.

I headed straight for the house, my mind in a turmoil It had all seemed senseless. Yesterday I was so clea about everything, and then Tocco leads me to this scene which is nothing but idiotic violence and brutality, and then a cheap Hollywood-type imitation of a Japanese whore to go through melodramatics with. Tocco had indicated that I would learn a lot, but all I seemed to find out was that people will go to any lengths to live out their fantasies. And while I had to admit I was being priggish since it wasn't too long ago that I myself was in that boat I resented being exposed to it again, especially so soon after I had come to terms with my own problem.

I marched into the dining room and made myself a cup of coffee, to sit and smoke and let my mind settle. decided to let the whole thing vanish from my memory and was just beginning to feel better about it when Tocco came in and sat next to me. He sat silent for a few minutes and then said, 'You should have paid her.'

His words were like picking at a scab and opening the sore again. 'For Christ's sake, Tocco,' I said. 'What was the point in bringing me there? She wasn't even a very good actress.'

'You fell for her, didn't you?' he said.

'Momentarily.'

'But she likes how she lives, and an affair with her would be very tricky. She would have to fit you in amidst the daily forest of cocks. And your ego wouldn't be able to withstand it.'

'Oh, what's the use of pursuing this?' I said. 'The masque is ended.'

Tocco looked at me. 'Oh, it wasn't a masque. She isn't acting.'

I rolled my eyes up in impatience.

He continued. 'She did that for seven years in Japan, and had become quite infamous, as well as making enough money to buy seventeen houses and some large plots of and. Her plan was to retire at age twenty-five and travel. She's a very intelligent and ambitious girl.'

'So, what's she doing here?' I asked.

'Last year, she went out for a walk and never returned. They found her sitting on a park bench talking to herself, totally incoherent, and practically catatonic. She just upped and burned out. They put her in an insane asylum, where she probably would have become a vegetable, but I heard of her situation, and considering her immense sexual accomplishments, I brought her here, where I rebuilt her home.'

My mouth dropped open. 'You mean she's crazy?' I asked.

Tocco smiled grimly. 'What's crazy?' he said. 'She is who she is. That's all.'

'But then she just goes on sucking off scores of men a week? I mean, where does that lead?'

He regarded me mockingly. 'Where does anything lead, Michael? The only difference between you and Bingo Katy is that she lives her condition fully, without any internal commentary constantly underlining her action. She is at one with herself, so she doesn't have to become anything. You are still thinking there is something more to be, even though you have overcome the notion that there is something more to know.' He paused a moment. 'You have to get past the stage where you know that you know.'

I took a deep sip of coffee. 'Tocco, you're fucking with my mind,' I said.

'Michael,' he answered, 'in light of the way Bingo Katy lives, in the face of the brute fact of her condition, and how she exists in it, without artifice, without guile . . . that she is able to be a beautiful hustling cocksucker and make no pretensions about it . . . how much weight do you give to that tawdry intellectual label by which you now mollify yourself, the notion of "male lesbian"?'

I looked at him a long while, our blank reflecting screens playing a thin edge of tension back and forth. And in that space, I saw that he was right. Even when I had gone most far-out, had indulged in living the wildes fantasies, always some part of my mind was watching comparing, filing. And when I had thought I had gone beyond thought, simply because there were no words in my mind at the time, my attitude and total posture treated my behaviour as mere illusion while the Observer inside me claimed to be the true reality. And yet, who was that Observer but another facet, another aspect of "I"?

Finally, I spoke. 'Who am I, Tocco?' I said.

He nodded. 'The other day you were asking who *I* was. Now your question is aimed in the right direction. I hope you don't make either the mistake of trying to answer it, or of ceasing to ask it.'

'But isn't metatheatre the maintenance of the self as audience for the play of the universe?'

'Not so long as you see self and universe as two separate things.'

I snorted. 'Are you going to take me on an "it is all one" trip?'

Tocco leaned back and gave me a long level look. 'When you have reached the outermost edges of your ego, and find it all to be desert; and then have gone to the centre of your being, and found it to be void, what do you do then?' He paused. 'Metatheatre is when the game of illusion is understood as reality, and reality is known as mysterious, and the mysterious is felt as familiar – the familiar being, of course, an illusion.'

It was hopeless. 'Tocco,' I said, 'I don't know anything anymore.'

He corrected me. 'You have never known anything, and for the first time you realise it. I/pray that you don't forget it too often.'

I was trying to elicit something from him, some word, some clue, but he remained impassive. I searched his face for some indication of his thought or feeling, and finally he said, 'Michael, I have said all that I can say to you. You have had all the experience you need, and you have awakened enough to keep you from going into blind alleys for extended periods of time. And now, since you don't know anything, everything will be new. Begin with where you are and start learning.' He heaved himself out of his chair and made as if to go. 'I may not see you for a while,' he continued. 'I have other areas of concern which demand my presence.' He took my hand, then concluded 'What you are looking for, you already have.' Then he turned and walked swiftly out of the room, leaving me bewildered and confused, but with a curious feeling of hope.

CHAPTER SIXTEEN

It was a small, dark room. Overhead a tiny red bulb threw the only light, a kind of musty shadowy glow. There was a double bed against one wall, a closet in the corner, and a small night table by the bed. We filed in silently and stood around for a moment in slight confusion. There was nothing else to do, so we took our clothes off.

Scotty was naked first. He stood a little over six feet tall, and his rich black skin glimmered in the red light. He had a wide face and large soft lips. Above them was a gentle moustache. Ellen took off her pants and turned to face us. Her thin mouth flickered around the edges of a smile. Her hard dancer's body stood erect and proud. She had small breasts with thick brown nipples. Her buttocks rode high and very round, white and covered with an almost invisible down. Next to her, Scotty arranged several joints and a folded paper of cocaine on the table.

Susan was next to stand nude, her gold hair flowing loose around her shoulders. She seemed all breasts and thighs, her tits hanging in rich fullness and her legs heavy and lush. Her naked cunt hung down. I took off my shirt and moved to stand next to them.

For a moment everything was poised at the edge. Then, in unison, we stepped forward and huddled together. We put our arms around one another's shoulders and leaned towards the centre. And suddenly, it felt as though we were one person. Scotty began to sway from side to side, and his motion spread to the rest of us. I could feel the mingled breaths envelop us. On either side, Susan's and Ellen's thighs pressed against my legs. I ran my hands down, and cupped each of their backsides in my palms. Electricity ran up into my shoulders. In front of me, Scotty's cock became hard and rubbed into my belly. I raised my face up and found his lips.

Our hands began to move all at once, while our bodies rolled and thrust into each other. We began to separate, and I found myself sinking down to plant my mouth on Ellen's breast. I was able to cover it entirely and sucked at it hard. I licked her nipple. Little shudders went through her and her knees buckled slightly. Scotty was down on Susan's breasts, licking the deep space between them, pinching each nipple with his thumb and forefinger. She let out low small moans.

I placed one hand between Ellen's legs and reached up under her cunt to grab her by the middle of her crotch. She leaned into it, and my thumb began to inch its way into her dry cunt. I moved it very slowly and soon I could feel the moisture begin to form, to lubricate the slot. I groped out and found my other hand slipping between Susan's cheeks to touch the lower part of her cunt. She arched her buttocks, and her cunt came sliding down on to my fingers. She was already very wet.

For a few moments we remained standing, Scotty and I working on each of the women's breasts and me with my finger in each of their cunts. Scotty grabbed my cock in his hand and began to massage it gently. The room filled with sighs and moans. A wave gripped us simultaneously and we rode it until it broke, our movements growing a little more frantic. And then we stopped, all of a sudden.

Susan and Ellen moved back and sat on the bed, and Scotty and I went to see about the dope. We brought the joints and the coke, and sat down with them. Scotty produced matches and I tore the cover off to use as a snifter. He lit the joints and I passed the paper around. For a while, we just sat quietly and got stoned, the grass producing mild billows in the space outside, and the cocaine melting the tension inside. Everything grew mellow and slow. The room seemed to close in to cover us.

I moved to put the roaches and the rest of the coke on the table. I turned back to find Ellen and Susan with their hands on each other's breasts. Scotty had leaned back, and the two women were gazing deeply into one another's eyes. They hung in balance for a moment, and then Susan lay back, drawing Ellen down on top of her. She lay with her knees wide apart and her feet touching, and Ellen's body lay straight into her. Their breasts mashed against each other. Susan's arms came up to encircle Ellen's neck, and Ellen reached down to stroke Susan's thighs. Their mouths hung open a fraction of an inch apart, and then their lips gently touched. A long sigh escaped Susan, and Ellen pressed her mouth forward, bringing her tongue out to lick at Susan's tongue. Their mouths began to move, pressing and pulling apart, nibbling and sucking. Simultaneously Ellen pressed her pelvis forward and the two cunts joined. Both let out a grunt of surprise, and Susan raised her legs to wrap them around Ellen's waist. Ellen tucked her pelvis under and started rhythmically to rub her cunt and bone and hair into Susan's naked lips.

They paused and disengaged. Ellen reared back and looked down into Susan's face, which now lay open and openly loving. Her mouth moved slowly, forming silent words. Her hands stroked Ellen's bottom. And her pelvis moved in tiny jerking thrusts. Ellen took a deep breath, then began sliding down. In one easy motion, from her ankles to her arse to her spine to her neck, she slipped down Susan's body until her face was at her crotch. And then, very deliberately, she leaned forward and brought her lips down to plant a tender kiss on Susan's cunt.

Susan groaned and flung her arms out to her sides. Ellen reached down under her and cupped each of her cheeks in her hands. She lifted, and brought Susan's cunt front and up, right to her lips, then dropped her head the tiniest bit, and began licking the thin slit between the outer lips. Susan's legs went higher and back, her knees towards her chest. Ellen reached up with her hands, and slowly peeled the lips back, exposing the inner cunt slowly and gently. It unfolded like a flower, revealing the wrinkled bud at the very centre. Ellen put out her tongue all the way in a long curve, and plunged it accurately and softly right into the heart of the opening. Susan shuddered and cried out softly. Without losing the rhythm, Ellen moved her tongue in and out, pressing her face all the way between Susan's thighs, then pulling back until only the tip of her tongue made contact. She reached in with her thumbs and pried the cunt completely apart, then leaned forward and started to lick it all over, outside, and on the outer lips, and in the crevices between them and the inner lips, and down into the hole again. Susan's cunt beame dripping wet, and Ellen put her entire right hand into it. She pushed until all five fingers were buried past the knuckles, and then made a fist. Susan cried out, 'Oh God have mercy!' as Ellen opened and closed her fist and ran her fingers over every part of the inside of Susan's cunt.

She pulled her hand out and glued her mouth to the sticky lips. Suction dents formed in her cheek as she pulled at Susan's insides like a vacuum. Susan began to writhe and vibrate, her entire pelvis moving in deep thrusts. Ellen hung in, catching the rise and fall of each cycle of Susan's inner excitement, in there with her, cunt eating cunt. From very deep inside, Susan began to come. It rolled in waves through her body and had her rippling like a worm. It seemed as though all her bones had melted and all her muscles gone soft. And nothing was left but skin and membrane, soft, delicate, sensitive pink membrane of cunt, oozing pearly drops and generating heat. As the climax came, Ellen was pumping her pelvis against the bed and her mouth became a living dance. Together they let out a great groan, and Susan's cunt bucked up and down, pouring vibration after vibration into Ellen's hot mouth.

They lay like that for a very long time, not moving.

Then Ellen moved up slowly and Susan held her cradled in her arms. They seemed almost light enough to float, and a faint glow shone around them. Scotty and I looked at each other, and smiled at the surprise in our eyes. We had become so enraptured by the sight of the two women making love, that we had forgotten ourselves and one another.

I looked at him and saw his face become lovingly tender. In an instant, all that we were capable of feeling for one another sang betwen us, and without I thought I moved into his arms. I felt very small and weak, and yielded myself to him in a vibrant passivity. As no woman ever could, he understood my mood. He embraced me tenderly, his hands slipping around my shoulders and running up and down my back. I laid my head on his chest while curling my legs up below me.

For a long time we sat like that, feeling the breathing and strength of one another's bodies, before he ran one hand down to cup my arse. All tension melted. My chest felt the heat of my beating heart and I heard myself moan as I grabbed his short curly hair and began kissing his throat, nibbling his chin and cheeks, finally bringing my mouth to his ear. Delicately I put the tip of my tongue into the opening, and with a shudder we were both suddenly grabbing each other hard. I felt the breath go out of me as he squeezed my ribs, and I took his whole ear in my mouth, tonguing it and moaning words which had no meaning.

A great sweeping desire went through me and his skin came alive to my touch. I gently pushed him back to the bed so that his body lay relaxed and unguarded before my eyes. My lips grew heavy and I leaned forward to glue them to his chest, feeling the hardness of bone and muscle in the wide space between his nipples. 'Is there anything special you want me to do first?' I whispered. He took my head in his hands and said, 'Only one thing: just don't rush.'

Then he was mine. I felt all my fear and uncertainty cut loose, leaving me with the actuality of his wanting me.

And I wanted to give him all that I had. I moved up and began to run my tongue over his cheeks and mouth, licking at his soft lips and feeling the tiny tremors of pleasure go through him. He was a great feast, every inch of him delicious and enticing, and I had an eternity in which to eat him.

There was no part of him I did not kiss or lap, and no part of him I did not experience with touching and smelling and being intensely aware of his reaction. Images flowed in and out of my head, but over everything was the act, the line of the movement, the unity of the dance. I got lost in the forests of his hair and emerged on the broad plain of his forehead. His eyes brought out a tenderness I didn't know I possessed. His jaw made me want to bite, and I gnawed at the hard skull beneath the warm flesh.

Like a dizzied explorer, I plunged down the canyons of his throat, and losing awareness of my awareness, dove to swim in the luxuries of his body, licking the long muscled arms and sucking at the delicate fingers, getting drunk in the aroma of his armpits, and rattling my brain in the rapid gallop over his rib cage. I rimmed his navel, sucking at his symbolic cunt, until he arched his back, and whimpering like a girl, opened his belly to my lips and teeth.

From there it was a mighty flight to his feet, where I lost myself in admiring the sheer sculpture of them. I lay there like a slave, but without the fantasies of subjugation, for all was beauty and relationship. What a simple joy to nibble at his toes, and run my tongue over the tender arch, and then to take the entire front of his foot in my mouth and suck it until I could feel the whorls of skin on each toe.

My heart sang as I now began the greatest journey, up his strong legs. He twisted and turned as I nipped his calves, and rolled to his side as I changed the mode and began to lick the skin up to his knees, then to the soft back part of the knees. He moaned at the edge between pleasure and inability to tolerate pleasure as I gently bit into that tender skin. And then succumbed totally by rolling over on his front.

Now the high, firm, sleek cheeks of his backside loomed as I sighted up his legs. With a twisting movement, I worked my face between his thighs which lay close together, and brought the tip of my tongue up the slot where his legs met, licking more and more sensitive skin until my tongue reached the valley itself, and I plunged hungrily between his buttocks. With a sigh, he opened his legs, and I fell into the musky smell of his arse, using my tongue to pry the globes of flesh apart and reach the desired hole.

Yet I contented myself with only a lick, and moved further, where his balls and cock lay pointing down from his crotch, and began to lick at his tool with wet hungry movements. His cock immediately became hard, and it was impossible to keep it pinned that way as it grew long. He arched his buttocks and his cock sprang forward pointing straight down towards the bed. For a long time I nibbled the soft underpart, nuzzling his balls, and then abandoned myself under him, worming my way beneath his legs so that I lay on my back, ready to take his immense cock into my mouth.

Then he was gone. All at once he rolled over and I found myself uncovered. I turned to him and found that Ellen and Susan had moved up and were gnawing at his crotch like hungry wolves. Their lips seemed to form one unbroken line of mouth as they sucked at the tip of Scotty's cock. I tried to move in with them, but there was no room. I tried to make contact with Scotty, but his eyes were closed and he was clearly being transported into another universe from the one I was sitting in at the moment. All of a sudden, a wave of despondency broke over me, and I felt totally left out, totally abandoned. The three of them had formed a closed circle and had dropped me without a second thought. I wondered if this were the price I paid for my particular form of sexual ambivalence. A man would use me as a woman, unless there were a real woman present. And a woman could use me as a man, unless there were a stronger man present. And I could not be a woman for a woman as much as a real woman could. So I was left with an interesting posture and a metaphysical hard-on, and no one in the species who would come to me fully.

I let the feelings of sorrow wash over me, but by now I was able not to let any mood destroy my sense of inner centre. And in a while I found myself growing quite cool. I sat way back on the bed, away from the three of them, and lit a cigarette. By this time Susan had moved up to sit on Scotty's cock and was riding her cunt on him hard, her buttocks jiggling like a water-filled balloon, while Ellen tried to get Scotty to work his fingers into her cunt. In an instant I attained an astonishing clarity. I saw the three of them as children playing at some absurd power game, each one trying to get closest to the heart of the action, and the heart of the action being no more than the place where the greatest activity and awareness took place. But they were not cooperating to create that centre, they were blindly following their urges, and then jumping around like tadpoles to wherever the ripples formed.

I saw what had happened with me. I had helped to form such a whirlpool where my mouth met Scotty's cock, and the two of them had jumped into it without insuring that I wasn't pushed out. And then another centre formed which itself broke apart, and Susan redefined it by playing one of the strongest cards, cunt covers cock, and in so doing, had pushed Ellen out, who was now trying to work up a centre of energy with her cunt and Scotty's fingers. From where I sat, I realised that a little bit of a conscious understanding of the process could allow us all to contribute fully and build an energy machine which would allow us all to take from it as much, and more, than we gave.

I was about to say something to them about it when I realised that words only destroy flow in such situations. Instead, I threw my cigarette away and moved down to cover Ellen's mouth with my own. Momentarily she pulled away, but I was insistent, and in a few moments her centre of energy moved away from her cunt to her lips. I poured my entire being into her through my tongue and breath, and she responded by sucking at my mouth like a child at a nipple, drawing me into her, licking at my lips, clutching at my hair with tiny clenched fingers.

As she came alive to our energy, Scotty's hand began to be able to discover her cunt. And now that she no longer had the panic that I had felt earlier, the fear of being left out, she could be indifferent to her cunt. His fingers moved slowly to her lips and, jerking with a life all their own, leapt to grasp her cunt with the suddenness of one grabbing for the silver ring on the carousel. She moaned as he touched her, and her moan reverberated into my mouth. She slid down a bit, and let her cunt open wide and wet to surround his fingers, covering them with the sticky fluid which signalled her growing passion.

The movement from Ellen's cunt electrified Scotty's hand and arm and body, and connected with the sensations where his cock lay buried in Susan's churning snatch. For a minute or so we hung suspended in that space, currents running from woman to woman through Scotty, and from man to man through Ellen, until we all felt the need for closer union.

I moved down to cover Ellen's body, and while Scotty held her lips wide apart, I moved my cock into her dripping hole. I felt the hardness of his fingers rub against my prick as I slid into her, and when I was totally imbedded he pulled his hand away. Ellen let out a deep sigh, and drew her legs up to let me enter her deeply.

There was a long moment in which there was no movement, and then we all opened our eyes and looked at each other simultaneously. Scotty and I were gazing at each other, while Ellen and Susan stared into one another's eyes. Then our gazes swung around, and Ellen and I matched eyes while Scotty and Susan locked looks. Finally, Susan and I saw our eyes, and Scotty and Ellen came together.

I felt as though my ego had dissolved and come together again, but now it had four faces instead of the one, and it was impossible for me to tell the difference between any of us. In the realest sense of the word, we were all one person. And anything one of us felt, all of us felt. The room seemed to hum with a soft libration, and we were lifted by a kind of psychic elevator which took us from the world of mundane perceptions to a world where everything was washed clean, and was always fresh, always being born, always coming into awareness of itself.

I moved back until I was raised halfway off the horizontal, and put my arm around Susan, who sat astride Scotty's cock. Scotty put one arm around Ellen. And suddenly it was as though Susan and I were fucking Ellen and Scotty, and they were a single male-female creature, with cock and cunt, as we were, and there was no difference between us. Simultaneously I was aware of Scotty and myself as men, and Ellen and Susan as women. And with that, the whole closet of costumes came tumbling open, and every last possible sexual role or attitude or fantasy sprang into view, washing away all labels and preconceptions and notions of what sex is about, while leaving untouched the simple reality of who we were in those bodies at that time and place.

And then we started to move. It was impossible to tell who was moving with whom, or how. It was as though we were a small boat on a large sea, and the sea began to roll under us. We had no violation and no choice but to sit there and allow ourselves to be moved. As soon as I understood that, I let all sense of responsibility go; I let all sense of thought go; I let all consciousness go. I moved into a state of awareness where there was no longer any split between *what* was happening and the *who* that it happened with. Everything was process.

Then the richness began. Feeling Ellen's superb and gooey cunt kissing my cock in wet sucking laps while watching Susan's cunt descend in shuddering sloppy roles on Scotty's radiating cock. Putting one hand on Ellen's chest to cup one nipple in my fingers, while leaning over to suck Susan's tit into my mouth. Watching Susan and Ellen come together and match the rhythm of their mouths moving into each other as counterpoint to the thrusts that Scotty and I delivered to each of their cunts. Looking deep into Scotty's eyes and flashing the male vibrations which danced back and forth between us.

Incredibly, it was possible to be male and female, to be bisexual, trisexual, and quadri-sexual; to be a male lesbian and a dirty old man and a timid little girl and a sadist and a transvestite; to be, in short, every last one of the roles which sprang from all my conditioning and training, which poured forth from my genes, which lay in everything my grandmother and grandfather had ever done; to be all the gods and goddesses and all the forms of the racial unconscious which continually works out its great drama in the pages of history and in the breath of every living moment; to be the entire earth, every mineral and animal called Michael. And then to know that I was the stars and the galaxies; to be, at once, the ridiculous panting sweating brave creature in that room and the entire essence of Being, all in one incredible blinding moment, and not to lose, in the glory of the moment, sight of the pain and shit and fear and decay and violence which made part of this strange animal called Michael. And then to know that I was not just Michael alone knowing this, for Susan and Ellen and Scotty shared the rhythms, were part of the same voyage, this blind seeing journey through time-space and eternity to feel their bodies rolling with mine and to sense that we were the same organism, like the children at the river's edge had been; and to watch our heads open, to know as solidly as I felt the bed under us that all of us knew the same thing, that all of us *were* the same thing; and as the realisation dawned and grew bright in me, our eyes all met at the centre and there a white glow appeared. A fire went on in our minds and we began to smile, not a smile that was attached to anything, but a smile that took its own shape around the curve of what was happening, as the energy balled up and gathered more energy to itself, and began to dance like a candle flame, and then to expand, until it engulfed us and filled the room and went beyond. My ears filled with the sound of a great choir and I saw that all of us were singing, no words, but a wide deep joyous sound that poured from our hearts and was nothing other than the primal sound, the first movement of creation, the surge of love.

And then we fell from the cliff edge, and holding one another, still moving and singing, we sailed out into the blue blue space, pulsing with love and freedom, until our bodies could contain no more, and simultaneously, with a great vanishing cry, we all came convulsing wildly into one another's arm, to fall into a great darkness where there was nothing but the silence, moving in immense mysterious ways that were, oh! so beautiful.

CHAPTER SEVENTEEN

We slept for a while, then got up to dress. There was an odd moment of awkwardness, the kind that might ordinarily have slipped by as unimportant. But after what we had just known with each other, it was impossible not to notice all the currents among us, even the tiniest. It is from these small discrepancies in the flow that the larger blocks to communication spring, yet we always seem to be so busy doing everything else other than paying attention to ourselves and one another, that we have lost the sensitivity to one another's changes which alone gives us a chance to avoid the hostility, confusion and pain which wracks all human society and culminates in war.

Scotty looked up. 'What's happening?'

'I don't know what to do next,' I said.

There was a short silence, then Ellen said 'It's like I feel we should stay together, but at the same time I feel the need to get back into myself.'

'That's it,' said Susan.

We all looked at each other. The vibration of our orgasm still throbbed in our bodies and in the air, and none of us wanted to lose that moment of blinding union. But it was gone, dead, only a memory now, and life pushes on, always. Yet, neither did we want to lapse into some mechanical routine where we would lose the fine edge of perception and empathy.

'Let's sit back down,' said Scotty, 'and ride this until it ends.'

We dropped our clothing and got back on the bed. I felt an urge to speak, but there was nothing to say. The others seemed to feel the same. So we looked at one another. In that time and space odd shapes began to form. The ways our eyes moved, and the subtle language of our bodies, and the thoughts which rolled through our minds, all were amplified in an obscure fashion, so that the room came alive with messages, but it was impossible to tell who was saying what. Then I became aware that there was no effort to communicate on anyone's part. Each of us was just sitting there doing his own thing, and letting expression flow as easily as water moves downstream. All at once there was a collective sigh of relief. Suddenly, there was nothing to do, nothing to say, nowhere to go. The moment was eternal, each moment, from moment to moment, and there is nothing but the constant awareness of it as it presents itself, always immediate, always fresh, always true.

Susan said, 'How long can we sustain it?'

I answered, 'The question is, how long will it sustain us?'

This was the final confrontation, after each of us had tried as hard as we could, after we had worked and suffered and striven to find some answer, some solution, the universe simply stepped in and let itself be known. Suddenly I saw my entire life as a child's game of attempting to alter the course of the inevitable. Here I was, a mortal, vulnerable animal, sitting on the edge of a great hunk of rock, hurtling at fantastic speeds and in dizzying interpenetrating cycles through a mysterious black universe, with no one anywhere to give the slightest hint as to who I was or what anything was about, and in this condition I had been attempting to exercise what I solemnly had called my free will. I took a mental photograph of the cosmos and breathed a silent prayer: 'Thy will be done.'

And with his impeccable timing, at that very instant,

212

Tocco threw open the door and stepped into the room. He was dressed in a white tunic with a short broadsword slung around his waist. Around his shoulders hung a purple cape. He wore a great golden helmet topped by a yellow plume, and on it emblazoned the initials: ISM. He let his impression sink in and then smiled. 'Allow me to introduce myself,' he said. 'I am Isador Tocco, MD, PhD, and Charlatan, currently Director of the Institute for Sexual Metatheatre.'

Susan looked at him open-mouthed. 'Tocco, you're stoned,' she said.

Tocco stepped in further and with a wave of his arm said, 'I see you people are having a seminar.'

Technically, that was true. After I had seen Tocco last, I hung around the grounds for a while, not knowing what to do. It seemed that no more lessons were forthcoming, and no one seemed particularly interested in involving me in anything. I wondered whether I was getting a brush-off, and started to think about leaving, when one morning I woke up with the feeling of being at home. Then I realised that I lived here; it wasn't merely a school. There was nowhere else I wanted to go. I thought of the world 'outside', with its stupidity and frigidity and lack of truth, and I knew that I was with people who had become like a family to me, or rather, like a tribe.

And then I understood what ISM was about. There was no research going on that was destined for publication in any journal. Everything that happened was geared to changing people in a radical way, mutating them so they lived their lives in a totally new manner. And once this happened, these people would want to stay with each other, doing all the simple ordinary things of life, but with heightened awareness and wider consciousness. Life here, after all, wasn't so terribly different in its forms than anywhere else. People ate and slept, talked and fucked, fought and loved. Rather it was a quality of richness, of fullness, that permeated everything; and this was the crucial change. I remembered an old Tibetan line about, 'The highest art is the art of living an ordinary life in an extraordinary manner.' Here there were no hidden games, our social roles were the stuff of our interaction and we knew it, so we learned to play the game well. And the ineffable, as always, was able to take care of itself. There was as much true mystical experience in one of ISM's orgies as in all the sit-up-straight meditation monasteries in the world.

That day, I went out into the garden with new eyes. And immediately everything changed. I met Susan on one of the paths, and it was good just to share time and space with her, with no compulsion for either of us to *do* anything; we had just to be, and let events shape themselves. In a way that was impossible before we became friends and spent days walking and sitting quietly making love. Even fucking was a different matter, like a dance which began with each of us in a separate centre of awareness, moving out of that and into a mutual circling which culminated in hard cock sinking luxuriously into the soft wet perfume of cunt, while our hands and eyes and legs and breasts continued their complementary movements, all building towards the moment when climax brought us erupting like a geyser into a sweet relaxation.

One day, while walking through the woods, we met Scotty and Ellen. They had been with Tocco for over a year, and the four of us liked each other at once. There was no immediate rush to intimacy, but over the weeks a closeness developed that was special without being exclusive. We met as four sometimes, or in combinations of two and three, so that no single pattern of relationship came to override all others. Then, one afternoon, over coffee and books, we all looked up at the same moment, and the awareness that the time had come was unmistakably present. We handled the details in a business fashion, with Scotty volunteering to take care of the dope, while I said I would take care of the room which, with no little irony, I fixed up like one of the places in the gay baths I used to visit in New York. When we entered that evening, there was a rich sexual tension enveloping us, but also a sense of beginning a serious experiment. Which went splendidly right up to the moment of Tocco's dramatic entrance.

Tocco lowered his great bulk on to the bed and looked at the four of us. 'What a lovely picture,' he said. 'Reminds me of when I was your age and first discovering the liberating effect of intelligence.'

I was shocked at the bitterness in his words, and stared at him to see whether it was actual or another bit of put-on. He turned and levelled his gaze at me and I saw nothing in his eyes but a fierce undefinable energy. 'Well, Michael, once again it seems to you that you have discovered something,' he said. 'What are you doing?' I asked. 'My usual task,' he answered, 'making sure you don't get swept up in the flush of realisation and begin to identify with the moment. That's a peculiar weakness of Scorpios: bringing so much passion to an event that it seems, somehow, more than real.'

The phrase rang in my head like a gong: 'more than real.' I looked up to answer and realised that perhaps ten seconds had gone by, with everyone watching me. 'It's impossible to be more than real, Tocco,' I said. Tocco leaned forward. 'Oh?' he said, 'and would you care to defend the metaphysics of that?'

I wanted to respond, but no words came out. The word-machine was totally non-functioning! My mind was broken. I tried to speak and made incoherent noises with my mouth. Tocco chucked me under the chin and turned to the others. 'He was such an articulate lad, and look at him now!' Scotty and Ellen laughed and Susan clapped her hands. Tocco had moved in, and with a few deft strokes had totally paralysed my personality. 'How old would you say you are now, Michael?' he asked. I closed my eyes. I felt as though I were about three. And just a few moments ago I had pretty much solved most of the problems of existence.

'Tocco,' I blurted out, 'you are a crazy-maker!'

'Also a sane-maker, Michael, don't forget that.'

'What do you want?' I asked. 'You helped me get to a

place I've wanted to be in for so long, and now that I am here you're trying to pull the rug out from under me.'

He leaned back, his eyes never leaving mine. 'You're like a child in a field of flowers, so busy running around to each one, trying to squeeze the essence from all of them, knocking yourself out rushing and never for a moment stopping, just to sit, and watch the entire view. You keep getting lost in a small tunnel of signification, forgetting that there are clouds and birds and the sun and all of time and eternity available too. Michael, you're ready to lean back and start pasting realisations in your scrap book. You keep missing the point, that the idea is only the theatre; the play is life, which cannot be measured by your mind.'

He rose off the bed and drew himself up to his full height and weight; his eyes flashed, and he was formidable. The others seemed to pull back from me, and I felt myself oddly isolated. The sense of strangeness, of an alien presence, pervaded me, and I sat gripped in an existential paranoia.

Tocco looked down and intoned, 'Come with me, Michael. Come to the place where there is no sleep, no lapsing back into hypnotic ease. Come out into the true void.' He paused, then added, 'You have only to open your eyes. The mystery stands always before you, dressed in forms you seem to recognise, speaking words you seem to understand.'

The ground gave way beneath me. I put my hands over my ears. 'Stop it, for God's sake, stop it,' I cried.

Tocco smiled a slow, malevolent grin. 'Why, Michael,' he said gently, 'you are the only one in the room.'

And then it seemed as though a precipice yawned in front of me. Beyond the cliff edge lay a canyon which had no bottom, and I felt myself drawn to its edge. I went like a sleepwalker and stood at the very edge and peered straight down. I knew that if I dropped, there would be no hitting earth ever again, that I would be always flying, always hung in the unsupporting air. And yet the incredible freedom of it pulled me forward, down. No attachment to anything ever again, never a holding on, an identifying. There would be no more reason, no more memory, no more fear.

I turned to look at the others, people with whom I had felt such a close and lasting union, they seemed far distant, like trees on a fast-receding horizon. My eyes implored theirs for help, for some sign, but nothing came back. I was totally alone, suspended between the inexorable pull into space and the crying need to have something or someone to hold on to.

'Death!' shouted Tocco. 'Accept your own death.'

And he slowly and majestically drew his sword. I watched him raise it above his head, reverse his grip, and point the gleaming tip at my chest. Something in the moment gripped me, and in a flash I saw the total meaning of everything. A rush of joy danced through me, and smiling, I flung my arms to my side and bared my breast.

'Then die, Michael,' Tocco said, and with a quick thrust crashed the sword into my chest. I felt a sharp pain and crumpled over.

And waited to die.

A long long time passed. From far away I heard titters. I wasn't dead.

I lifted my head and looked up at Tocco. In his hand he held the squashed remnants of his sword. The thing was made of papier-mâché.

The slow burning sensation began in my feet and rose up my body like mercury in a thermometer. I felt my face go beet-red, and I looked around at the others. They all had their hands over their mouths, trying to suppress their giggles. I could feel my face turning into an angry mask. And then Tocco just broke out. Peal after peal of laughter roared from his belly. Scotty let out a high-pitched whinny, while Susan and Ellen laughed silently into their lips.

There was no way to sustain my anger, and it lapsed into a sullen pout. I sat there until their mirth subsided, and then Tocco, tears in his eyes, clapped one hand on my shoulder. 'Oh, Michael! You'll never make it at this rate!'

I looked up sharply. He sobered instantly, and making a sweeping gesture which took in the entire Institute, said, 'You'll never make it this way.'

I had no time to react to his enigmatic statement before Susan's voice cut in: 'Why, he's not even bored yet.'

Tocco spoke to her sharply. 'He doesn't understand the terms in that way yet. Don't confuse him.' To my surprise I heard her say quite contritely, 'I'm sorry.'

Tocco was about to add something when, suddenly, a giant bell began clanging. The four of them jumped up in haste, looking at each other in alarm.

'What's that?' I asked.

'Probably the police,' said Tocco. He turned to Scotty. 'I knew we were getting too conspicuous in the village. They must have begun watching us through binoculars.'

'What happens now?'

Tocco turned to reassure me. 'That's the first alarm. It means we have five minutes.'

'Can we bluff it out?' asked Ellen.

'No,' said Tocco, 'we could never get rid of the dope and the tapes and the movies and photos in time. We'll have to pack it in.'

We all looked at each other for a moment. 'Come on' he said, and began moving out of the door. 'We'll go through the elevator in my office and then jam it from the bottom.'

We started off at a brisk pace down the hall, Tocco's cape flying behind him, his helmet bobbing up and down, holding his crumpled sword to the fore. The four of us followed after, cocks bobbing and breasts bouncing, clutching our clothing to our chests. Like a man at the point of impact in an auto accident, I saw the headlines on tomorrow's newspapers, and photos of us, with little black strips to cover our genitals and nipples. It all seemed to fit.

We turned a corner and were in clear sight of Tocco's

office, when six cops came tumbling down the hall from the other direction.

'Fuck!' said Tocco.

He turned left and bolted into one of the rooms, us piling in after. Even in that instant I could see the cops' eyes go wide as they saw Ellen and Susan scrambling past. It halted them for a moment, and one of them yelled out, 'She's got no hair on her cunt!' The moment's delay in their charge helped us, and we got into the room and bolted it behind us.

'We take our chances in the woods,' said Tocco, and in the next minute we were flying across the lawn, heading for the protection of the trees.

Tocco ran amazingly fast. And before I had gone three-quarters of the way to cover, he had disappeared. Scotty and Ellen flashed in after him. Susan veered slightly to the left and vanished behind a tree. I tried to turn to follow her, but I was already plunged in a different direction.

I ran for five minutes, stumbling and banging my shins against tree barks, until I fell totally exhausted to the ground. I lay there gasping for a minute, and gradually came back to myself. The wood was uncannily silent, and almost pitch black. I heard no noises of people running and thanked my destiny that we had escaped.

And then I sat up with a start. There were *no* sounds. Where were Susan and Tocco and Scotty and Ellen? I began to call out, then realised that would only give me away to any police in the area. I got up silently and dressed. I had only a shirt, trousers and shoes. My socks were somewhere in the house. And the night was chilly.

I began walking, knowing I would sooner or later come to a road or to the stream, and find my way back to civilisation. If I could get back to New York, I had friends who would let me crash with them until I got something together.

I walked most of the night and came to the main road. It was almost dawn and few cars passed. I crouched down in the shadows of some bushes and waited. Soon a produce truck came lumbering up the road. I jumped out and hailed the driver, who came to a suspicious halt.

'Going into the city?' I asked.

He wavered a moment and I plied him with my friendliest manner. 'I'll ride in the back, OK?' I said. And before he could think of his response, I moved off and jumped into the rear opening. A moment passed, and then I heard the gears grind.

I sat on some crates and chewed at a head of cabbage as we rolled off, and wondered what had become of the others. I put my hand down to my crotch and grabbed my cock for comfort. I felt empty, untroubled, and sad.

In a while, the sun rose and the smells of dawn blew through the truck. 'We'll meet again, Tocco,' I said to the passing fields.

By the next afternoon, I was in the city. I had enough money for a room and food for a week, and then it was looking for another gig. I became depressed and headed out to one of the favourite cruising bars uptown. The crowd was the same as it had always been. But somehow, I had changed. Everyone seemed dull, lifeless, asleep. They looked as though they were going through some endless meaningless dance, without knowing why, or even aware that they had a choice. Or did they have a choice?

I flashed a young couple who were looking to add excitement to their marriage, and after the preliminaries, we went to their place. She was attractive in a thin sort of way, and he was more interested in watching than participating. In fact, after a while he asked if I minded if he took out his movie camera. I gathered that after their guests left, he got his jollies by having her suck him off as he watched the movie of her making it with another person. I went through the ritual and enjoyed it, because she had a friendly cunt, the kind that is very soft and accommodating. And she had a way of throwing her ankles over my shoulders so that I practically penetrated to her navel that I liked.

But there was no Tocco to come in and make trenchant remarks on the follies of the human condition. There was no Kate to look into my face with eyes of infinite pain and compassion. There was . . . there was no Susan. And for a while I became sentimental, and then realised that it wasn't the people I was missing, it was what they did.

I finished fucking the girl and lay back, and for the first time really looked at the people I was with. And I wanted to say something, somehow to make us more comfortable with each other. But they seemed content. So I blurted out, 'I'm uncomfortable, and it's got nothing to do with you two. I just . . .'

They exchanged glances which said, 'Oh no, I hope he's not going to get serious and make a scene of some sort.' And then I knew what was lacking. These people were frivolous. To them, life was a tedious game to be spiced with tricky adventures. They were not serious people. And I don't mean sombre. But serious. Concerned with living life to its fullest. Which, I realised, didn't mean having the most experiences, but having the greatest awareness. Of really taking care of observe what was happening, whether it be a sunset, or a piece of music, or fucking someone in the ear. It didn't matter. It was the quality of approach that was important. And that was what Tocco and his people were all about! They all had the same sense of approaching life with a lusty reverence. And they were gone, and I hadn't the slightest idea how to find them.

I sat up. I would begin looking right away! The couple seemed startled. 'Aren't you going to spend the night?' he said. I looked back. The woman was leaning back and fingering her cunt and smiling into my eyes. My resolve wavered. Maybe I was being an idiot. Maybe my problem was that I was too serious. Maybe . . .

My mind spun like a top. I looked up. 'I'm really confused,' I said, 'I don't know what I'm doing.'

The woman came over to me. 'I have something for confusion,' she said, and put her wide hot mouth full over my already stirring cock. And as I felt her tongue begin to lick the head of it, and her cheeks cave in as she sucked, I watched her husband change the lenses on his camera to a close-up. And as my cock hardened and bulged deep into her throat, as her bottom began to roll and gyrate on the bed, as the smell of her wet cunt once again began to fill the air, her husband wound up his camera and came all the way in for a full close shot.

I lay back in temporary bliss and promised myself that I would begin my search for Tocco . . . tomorrow.